About the author

Mark was a Hampshire police officer for thirty years, retiring in 2011, as a detective chief inspector. In the police, his particular interest was the control and management of sexual and violent offenders, and the investigation and support for vulnerable victims, such as domestic and child abuse victims. Mark was fascinated by the inter-relations between dangerousness and vulnerability.

Mark started writing books which explore this, when he was diagnosed with multiple system atrophy. Zodiac is his second novel. MSA cruelly changed the life Mark loved. We utterly admire the way he faced this challenge, to write the books he knew he had inside him.

Mark died in December 2019. He is missed so much, by so many people, and we are very proud that his voice and his work lives on in his books. To find out more, visit www.markashthorpe.co.uk.

Debbie Ashthorpe

By the same author

Chameleon

Zodiac

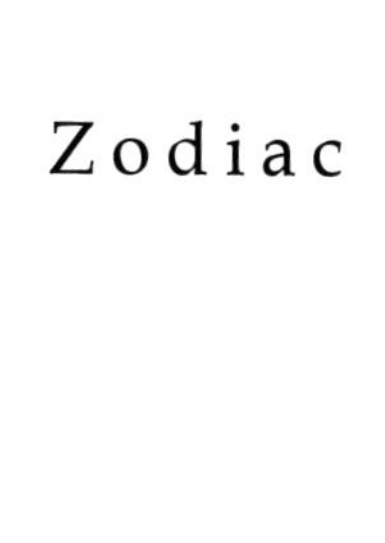

Mark Ashthorpe

Zodiac

Pegasus

PEGASUS PAPERBACK

© Copyright 2020
Mark Ashthorpe

The right of Mark Ashthorpe to be identified as author of
this work has been asserted by him in accordance with the
Copyright, Designs and Patents Act 1988

All Rights Reserved

No reproduction, copy or transmission of this publication
may be made without written permission.
No paragraph of this publication may be reproduced,
copied or transmitted save with the written permission of the
publisher, or in accordance with the provisions
of the Copyright Act 1956 (as amended).

Any person who does any unauthorised act in relation to
this publication may be liable to criminal
prosecution and civil claims for damage.

A CIP catalogue record for this title is
available from the British Library

ISBN-9781910903 37 7

Pegasus is an imprint of
Pegasus Elliot MacKenzie Publishers Ltd.
www.pegasuspublishers.com

First Published in 2020

Pegasus
Sheraton House Castle Park
Cambridge CB3 0AX England

Printed & Bound in Great Britain

Dedication

This is for my marvellous and talented family, who continue to astound me with their amazing talent and success. My daughters have turned me into an unashamedly proud father. So, this is for the remarkable "plate spinner" Debbie; Victoria known as Vicky everywhere but home; Abigail aka Abs; and Emily, known at home as Emi B or Mrs B.

Acknowledgements

I am indebted once again to my "first readers", Tanya and Helen as well as Simon for their help and input. I am grateful also to Margaret, Stephy and Nicola for their support and feedback, post editing. I am very lucky to have such a group of readers to support me; it would be impossible to do it on my own. I'd also like to thank all of our tremendous friends whose help, along with carers and health professionals make living possible.

Prologue

I've been seeing Julie on and off for quite some time now, since I saved her daughter, Kelly-Ann's life. Julie was naturally very grateful, and she was undoubtedly an extremely attractive woman. And therein lies the rub; I like Julie a lot but I can't properly be with Julie because I want desperately to be with her daughter. I love her, I adore her, and I think she loves me as well. I dream about her, but I know I can't have her, not in the way that I really want. So, I see Julie and consequently I hope to have opportunities to see Kelly-Ann. I have to be careful, though, one thing for sure is that I don't want to go back to prison. In my life I am always professional, pleasant and helpful. I have a job, a house, I don't drink to excess or do drugs, I have a stable relationship, so, looking at all the criminogenic factors — you can tell I've been reading up on the subject — I am seen as a low risk of reoffending. That gives me wriggle room, I'm off Paul Evans' radar but I want it to stay that way.

So, I am incredibly careful how I behave around Kelly-Ann, but I also take my opportunities when they come; if there is any chance for accidental or incidental physical contact, I take it. Just the feeling of brushing up against her is electric, I'm left almost speechless if our fingers touch; we sometimes sit closely on the sofa and I'm in heaven. It's not ideal though; I'm no saint, but it will have to do.

Julie trusts me completely, and she's right to. I would never do anything to harm Kelly-Ann, and before you say it, I know that includes sexual contact, so I will never touch her in a sexual way. That doesn't stop me dreaming, though. I have read a lot about minor attraction and I know that most people convince themselves that what they are doing is not only harmless, but actually mutually beneficial to the child as well as the adult. I don't kid myself; I know the harm it causes but that's only because of the social stigma and unevolved social attitudes. Because of this, I stay hands off, and out of prison, keeping my love and my sexual preferences well hidden.

Chapter 1

They lay in bed entwined, luxuriating in the exquisitely warm, comforting feeling of peace and security. From her second-floor luxury apartment, they could look out over the marina through the vast picture window. The development of quayside properties with moorings for the really wealthy was nestled on the west bank of the river Lees, with Leeston town on the east bank. You can cross the river either by a road bridge outside of town or by the small chain-link ferry at the hard, in the middle of town. From their vantage point, they admired the natural wonder and beauty of the magnificent sunrise above the town across the water. The mist-enshrouded sailing boats were eerily reflected in the shimmering water. It was autumn and the pale sun made the sky a surreal hue on a giant artist's canvas.

Sue Taylor's flat was a legacy of her failed and abusive marriage. The year before, Sue had left her surgeon husband after he'd seriously assaulted her, and she had vowed never to fall under anyone's control again. Detective Inspector Sue Taylor and Detective Chief Inspector Steve Jones had met on the April Miles abduction investigation six months ago and had quickly hit it off. Sue had been immediately drawn to Steve's gentle and thoughtful nature; he was attracted to her looks, her determination and her energy.

Sue Taylor was in her mid-thirties, slim and attractive with short, blonde hair. She ran the Western Area Criminal Investigation Department from the police station in Leeston Forest, Southshire and she was very well thought of by the people she was responsible for. She had the rare combination of being intelligent and sharp, as well as warm and caring. The people who worked for Sue were often more than happy to go the extra mile, just for her.

Steve looked good for his age. He was a little over forty, slim and fit and — importantly from Sue's point of view — unmarried. Having both had previous bad experiences, Sue and Steve did not get together immediately. When they first met, they had danced around the issue, texting and e-mailing each other, flirting, for several months but in the end, they gave in to the inevitable and started seeing each other.

They had decided to kick-start their relationship by getting far away from it all and spending some time together. They drove down to the French Alps via the Channel Tunnel. They reasoned that if they could cope with this length of time in each other's company, then it might be worth giving it a go. The other option being to just drift into a relationship whilst still juggling work commitments. Neither thought the latter a great proposition.

The eleven-hour drive gave them an opportunity to become comfortable with each other, so by the time they arrived at their chalet, they felt as though they'd known each other for years. The winding roads and hairpin bends they navigated as they climbed into the mountains added to the thrill of being somewhere extraordinary. It was late summer, and they had rented a charming chalet in a small village three quarters of the way up one of the mountains abutting Alpe D'Huez. The view from the balcony on the first-floor living room was awe inspiring. Not only were they surrounded by the sheer majesty of the adjacent summits, but there was also a direct view of a magnificent waterfall tumbling down the mountainside.

As clouds swept an electric storm into the valleys, there was a primeval sense of being consumed by the natural forces of the region.

The week Sue and Steve had spent together was perfect, and the ideal way to cement the start of a relationship. Walking and cycling, dining and making love was also the perfect remedy to help them forget their busy and stressful lives.

Unfortunately, all too soon they had found themselves coming back to reality via the Channel Tunnel to the whirlwind that was the lives that they both led.

Having times like this together, watching the sunrise, were precious. It was seven a.m. one Sunday when they heard Sue's phone start to ring. Sue groaned. She was on call and she knew that being contacted early meant nothing but bad news.

She answered the phone and, as expected, it was the control room sergeant. "Good morning, I assume you have some bad news for me?" she said as brightly as she could.

"Morning ma'am, sorry to disturb you, but a body has been found by a dog walker. It was buried in a shallow grave on the river Lees footpath, eastbound towards Leeston marina. Detective Sergeant Smith, the duty DS, is there, and he asked us to call you out."

"OK," muttered Sue, still waking up.

"Shall I tell him you're on your way?" asked the sergeant.

"Yes, I'm not far away, I'll meet him there in twenty minutes."

Sue went back to the bedroom where Steve was lying awake.

"Job?" said Steve.

"Dead body."

"OK, call me if you need anything." Steve murmured, rolling over, almost immediately asleep.

Sue quickly showered and dressed and was wide awake, buzzing with curiosity as she left. She had her "go" bag ready with everything she needed to start an investigation. She knew the area she was going to, having walked there many times. It was a mostly overgrown footpath, a metre wide, skirting the waterfront towards the marina. It was used just by locals and dog walkers and was seemingly quite remote and quiet.

She had no detail yet, but her mind was buzzing with questions to be answered. The main question though, was whether it was a suspicious death or not.

Sue parked her Mercedes convertible in the nearest car park to the footpath, grabbed her bag and strode purposefully towards the pathway. She turned right and could see that the sun was still rising and the scenery across the water was bathed in the early morning light. But Sue now had a job to do and had no time for the view.

When she'd gone a hundred metres or so, she found a uniformed officer posted, standing next to police tape tied across the path, to stop any unauthorised person walking through the potential crime scene. She was logged into the scene by the young officer whom she recognised but didn't know, then walked further along where she could see her favourite Detective Sergeant, DS Paul Smith.

Straight down to business, she said, "Morning Paul, what have we got?"

"Morning ma'am, not good news, I'm afraid. Looks like a young boy, maybe ten or so, by the looks of him. He was found buried in that ditch there by a dog walker. It seems he had been covered, hidden in a shallow grave." Sue looked at the body of a small, thin boy with short, sandy hair. He was lying half in and half out of the ditch.

"How did the body get into that position if it was buried?"

"The lady's dog, a large black Labrador, caught the scent and started digging. The owner tried to call the dog away, but the dog kept digging until it found the body. The dog then started to drag the body out, but the dog walker got his lead on and pulled him away. She then called us."

"Thanks Paul; do you know if he's got any injuries?"

“I haven’t examined him; he’s obviously dead and I didn’t want to disturb any potential forensic recovery.”

“Quite right.” One of Sue’s pet hates was TV shows with investigators trampling all over crime scenes and destroying evidence. Some detectives tried to emulate their TV heroes, but this was something Sue was very hot on and her staff knew that the preservation of evidence was crucial. From her experience, the recovery of minute blood spots or tiny fibres can link suspects to crimes which they may otherwise get away with.

Paul continued, “I’ve called for a forensics team and I’ve cordoned the area off. I sent someone home with the dog walker because she was in shock. I also asked them to take a statement from her.”

Sue was thinking hard “He doesn’t look decomposed, so may not have been dead long. I’ll talk to the crime scene manager and arrange for a pathologist to come out.”

“Paul, can you call out someone to scope the area for any potential CCTV or witnesses. Also look at the potential for house-to-house enquiries. Get hold of me when the pathologist arrives; I’m calling this a murder investigation, so I’ll set up an enquiry at Leeston.”

“Yes ma’am,” said Paul.

Sue walked back to her car as the forensics team arrived in the car park. She spoke to the crime scene manager, Dave Johnson, quickly briefing him about the circumstances. They agreed the strategy for a forensic sweep around the vicinity of the body, but they would wait for the Home Office pathologist before touching it.

She got into her car, lowered the soft top, then headed towards her office in Leeston police station. The station was an ugly 1970s block, built with an inner courtyard and completely out of keeping with the character of the town, which was an historic, picture postcard, market town.

She sat in her office, having arranged a call out for a squad of detectives. She then called the duty Detective Chief Inspector to update him on the morning's events. It just so happened that the duty DCI was currently asleep in her bed.

Sue spoke in a business-like fashion to Steve Jones, despite having shared a bed with him not long before: "Steve, it looks like a murder. A young boy has been found buried in a shallow grave along the footpath near the marina; the fact that there have been efforts made to conceal the body makes it suspicious for me."

"I agree," said Steve.

"I've called a Home Office pathologist to go to the scene. I'm setting up an incident room at Leeston; shall I meet you here?"

"Yes please, I'll get there as soon as possible."

Chapter 2

At Manningsbrook Children's Home everyone was getting up and starting their day. The home was run by the local authority and all the children were in the care of social services. The day staff, Luke and Sophie, were in the habit of getting the kids up and getting them to make breakfast. In all there were six staff members working different shifts; Luke and Sophie had started at six a.m., taking over from the manager, Alan, who had stayed overnight. Making breakfast is quite a task but it was good for the kids to have a bit of responsibility.

There were eight children in the home: six boys and two girls, ranging from seven to thirteen years of age. There had to be two staff on site at any one time during the day and one at night. Alan often volunteered to stay overnight for which the others were grateful.

The house was on the outskirts of Leeston Town and was a huge detached Victorian house, set in an acre of grounds. The house would once have been elegant and charming but was now falling apart. It had been recently decorated in standard local authority pale blue with accompanying fire doors and office space so, inevitably the house didn't have a homely feel, it felt antiseptic, sterile. There was ample recreation space and large communal areas, though. The house was not lovely any more, but it was functional.

Everyone was sitting around the two kitchen tables, except for Aaron Wheeler. Luke quickly looked in his bedroom, but there was no sign of him. Luke put his head round the kitchen door, calling out "Anyone seen Aaron?"

The rest of the kids looked at each other, then shook their heads.

Luke became suspicious, "When did anyone see him last?"

Again, a collective silence. "Come on, where is he? Who saw him last?"

Jade Matheson, the oldest of the girls, and a very recent arrival said, "I heard someone say that he went to something called the 'Zodiac Club'. He didn't come back."

Luke turned to the others. "What time did he go?"

Finn Oliver, the unofficial leader of the group, glared at the others for a moment, then said "He went out on his own, yesterday after lunch. None of us know where he went."

Luke was more concerned about Aaron going missing than he might normally be with some of the kids. Children in care often run away. A lot of them run because of "pull" factors such as wanting to see siblings, parents or friends where they come from. Others run because of "push" factors such as bullying or just not wanting to be there. Aaron was more concerning as Luke didn't know of any push/pull factors and he had no known family. He was small and vulnerable and didn't normally abscond. Unlike some of the others who ran away frequently, Aaron was timid and had never disappeared before.

Luke picked up on what Jade had just said, "What's the Zodiac Club?" Although, for some reason the name Zodiac Club rang a bell somewhere in his mind, he couldn't place why.

Finn again replied, "Never heard of it, I think she made it up," looking across at Jade, who glared back.

"Liar, I heard you say it!" she said.

"You're the liar, you don't know anything."

Luke intervened, "Calm down, you two. You're not helping anyone by arguing."

The two continued to stare at each other, while the others all stayed silent.

"Look if anyone knows where he is, you have to say, because I'm calling the police."

They all looked at each other but remained quiet.

"All right, have it your way, I'm calling the police now."

Luke was thinking about Aaron. He was such a small child and hadn't been at the home very long. He'd never caused any trouble. Luke understood that he had been accommodated because he'd lost his parents in a car accident and had no other family. He wondered why Alan, the manager, hadn't noticed him missing last night at bedtime, if Aaron really went out yesterday afternoon.

Luke told Sophie, the other carer, what he was doing, then went to the office to report it to the police.

Chapter 3

The two men stood in the shabby lounge of the sparsely furnished, grubby two-bedroomed flat. The flat was above a small row of shops in the middle of the "Trees" council housing estate near Leeston town centre. The shops were in Hazel Avenue, which was the largest road dissecting the estate. They comprised the usual mixed bag of outlets in modern English shopping centres; a charity shop, a fish-and-chip shop, a betting shop and a late-night convenience store. The windows of the shops were all shuttered because of the amount of vandalism occurring and the frequency of break-ins. An unblinking eye, a lone CCTV camera perched on its pole, testament to the need for security.

The flats were all linked to the shops below, but access could only be gained via the rear passageway leading to iron steps up to a concrete balcony, which reeked of urine. Of the four flats, three were rented out through the local authority to younger people, making the block a magnet for drink and drugs. The fourth flat belonged to the owner of the fish-and-chip shop, Dave Fenwick. The 'Happy Chippy' was a thriving business but the flat was always left vacant. The two men stood in the lounge, apparently not noticing the faint odour of mould mixed with stale alcohol and tobacco.

One of the men, Dave Fenwick, was in his mid-fifties, short and fat, balding with black greasy hair. He looked like an English Danny de Vito. He always smelled of the fat that he used to cook in his shop. His grey trousers, collared shirt and cardigan were as greasy as he was, rarely finding their way to a washing machine.

By contrast the other male was six-foot-tall and slim, smart but casually dressed, with a military bearing. He could have been anything from forty to sixty. He was known to Fenwick as Capricorn, a leading member of a small secret group who all had code names taken from star signs, to help ensure anonymity.

Capricorn looked furious. "What the hell went on yesterday, Pisces?"

Pisces stuttered. "I… I don't know. The Zodiac Club was all going as usual then the boy just seemed to stop breathing. There was nothing we could do. It was horrific, we had to bury the body."

"How did he die, what did you give him?"

"Nothing unusual."

"Who else was here last night?"

"Libra and Scorpio. Oh, and that Finn boy who brought him here."

"Bloody hell, so we're vulnerable!"

"But no one will find him soon, he's well hidden," said Pisces, defensively.

"Oh, do you think so? He's already been found! A dog walker found the body. The local Detective Inspector has already started an investigation!"

Pisces looked terrified, "Is there anything you can do?"

"I'll make some calls; I'll see if I can spike the investigation. We need everyone on board, get all the members together for an urgent meeting, here, tonight at eight. It's a three-line whip."

"All right," said Pisces.

They both went their separate ways, Pisces to the shop to start getting ready for the lunchtime trade and to contact the other members of the Zodiac Club.

Chapter 4

Luke nervously telephoned Alan Rogers, the care home manager; he didn't know how he would react to the news of Aaron going missing.

Alan took it remarkably well, saying that he would come straight away to handle the police report. Luke was relieved and happy with this, because Alan was very experienced and knew the kids better than he did, having worked at Manningsbrook for many years. Alan was in his fifties, genial and unflappable; never having any children of his own, he cared deeply about the children in the home. He looked like a favourite uncle, which was the approach he took with the children in his charge.

By the time Alan arrived, a fever of speculation had started, and rumours of where Aaron had gone were proliferating. Finn was tight-lipped and told everyone to just shut up about Aaron, he was going to be fine.

When the uniformed police officer arrived, she was ushered into the manager's office and the door was shut.

Alan Rogers did not know the officer, so he introduced himself first. "Sorry to bother you on a Sunday morning but one of the kids, Aaron Wheeler, has gone missing. I'm not too worried because he's pretty streetwise, and he's gone and come back before. He hasn't any real worries as far as we know, I can only think that he'll come back when he's ready."

"Have you checked any likely places that he could be?" said the officer.

"Yes, I've had a drive around likely places but now that it's later I'll phone a few of his school friends' parents. I've prepared the missing report for you."

Because children often went missing from the care home, it was practice for them to have pre-prepared missing persons reports to save time gathering information.

The officer scanned the report, then remarked, "It says here he's not been reported missing before."

Alan hesitated, then said, "No, he's always come back before we've needed to report him. I think he likes wandering."

"If I can take this photo, we'll return it when he's found."

The officer left and Alan looked relieved. He could do without this trouble and he'd had to come in on his day off to help sort the mess out. Still, it had to be done.

Chapter 5

Sue answered the phone in her office, "DI Taylor."

"Hello Sue, it's Detective Chief Superintendent Irvine here."

Scotty Irvine was the most senior detective in the force but didn't like Sue and was something of her nemesis; the feeling was mutual, and they often clashed.

"Morning sir, are you calling about the murder investigation? I haven't yet got much of an update; we're just getting started."

"That's why I'm calling. It sounds very unlikely to be a murder doesn't it? From what I've heard it's the body of a missing kid from the children's home. He probably died of hypothermia not realising how cold it was last night."

Sue was nonplussed, "What missing child, I've not heard anything about this?"

Scotty Irvine continued, "You need to get a grip Sue, I shouldn't have to be the one to tell you. Anyway, I've cancelled your pathologist, and told the forensics team to finish up. Thankfully, just in time to save you wasting the force a fortune. Don't spend any more time on this, it all seems quite straightforward, a sad but not suspicious death. Your DS at the scene agrees with me."

As Irvine unctuously continued, Sue felt her hackles rising but she managed to remain calm. This was typical of the man, to use his power to belittle and humiliate her.

"But it looked like someone tried to conceal the body, though."

"Not very well, eh?"

"All right sir," Sue responded stiffly, then hung up the phone. Sue wasn't giving up that easily, though. He wasn't going to get away with hijacking her enquiry, but she wondered where he got his information from.

Her next call was to Paul Smith, her DS at the scene. Without preamble she said, "Paul, I know the detective chief super has spoken to you. I don't care what you've been told, just make sure forensics do a thorough job. This may or may not be a murder, but we only get one chance at getting the forensic evidence."

"I've already spoken to the crime scene manager and he agrees. Murder or accidental death, they'll do a proper job. Shame about the Home Office Forensic pathologist, though. It looks like we'll just get the hospital pathologist, with probably no experience of murders."

"No problem Paul, you and I will go to the post mortem to make sure nothing's missed. I'm not taking any chances with this, despite Scotty Irvine."

At this point Sue saw one of the local uniformed constables waiting at the door.

"Come in Sally," said Sue.

"Ma'am, I thought you'd like to know about this straight away, so I came here directly from taking the report."

"What's that?"

"I hear that a child's body has been found near the marina; well, I just took a missing person report from a local children's home, Manningsbrook, I wondered if it was connected."

"So I just heard from headquarters," Sue said acerbically.

"Anyway, it's possible the missing child is your body. His name is Aaron Wheeler, he's seven years old, small and thin, short, sandy hair."

Sue pictured the body she had just seen. "Could well be the same boy. HQ have already linked the two events. They've assumed it was an accident, probably hypothermia. I am still looking into the death, though, as I'm not happy to just make assumptions. Thanks for coming to me with this, Sally."

Sally left, happy that Sue would be looking into the case.

Sue sat at her desk deep in thought. She was going to defy Scotty Irvine, which was a risk. As she was thinking about what to do, Steve came into the office. "I had a call from DCS Irvine, he tells me there's no murder squad? Maybe we can go for coffee?"

Sue looked closely at Steve to gauge his reaction to what she was about to say, "I don't think so, I'm not sure yet what's going on, I'm still looking into it."

“Oh, sorry, I was under the impression that it’s clear now what happened.”

“Well it’s not clear at all, that’s just Irvine interfering. What I don’t get, is how he knew about the missing boy before I did. The officer taking the report came straight here.”

Steve had already lost interest in the dead child. “What does it matter?” Steve started but stopped short when he saw Sue’s face, which was like thunder. “OK, I’ll go now, call me if you need anything. Let me know how the post-mortem goes.”

Chapter 6

A mobile phone rang in the Happy Chippy. Dave Fenwick answered after looking at the caller ID: it was Capricorn using his burner phone; an unregistered, untraceable, pay-as-you-go mobile phone which they all had for security reasons, "Hello Capricorn, how did it go?"

Capricorn said, "I think that the investigation has been spiked, it's no longer ongoing."

"That's good news. I called the others; they're all nervous but agreed to meet tonight."

"So they should be. They've got to understand that we're all in this together. If any of this gets out, we're all sunk."

Pisces said, "I take it that there'll be no Zodiac Club today."

Capricorn said, "You are joking! There won't be any, not for a while, we need to keep our heads down for a bit."

Pisces had a thought, "What about the boy, Finn?"

"Get him to come here at seven, I want to speak to him."

The post-mortem was set for two p.m. It was going to take place at the city hospital mortuary, which was the closest to Leeston. The Manningsbrook care home manager, Alan Rogers, went to the hospital mid-morning to identify the body. Alan got tears in his eyes when he identified Aaron Wheeler. The boy looked peaceful and angelic lying in the viewing room. Alan was clearly distressed at seeing one of his charges like this.

The police officer who monitored the viewing took a statement from Alan who left swiftly afterwards.

When asked, Alan repeated his assessment of Aaron; a streetwise boy who often went off, but always returned so was never reported missing.

DI Taylor and DS Smith arrived at the mortuary in good time to brief the pathologist, Rory Pearson. Sue had met Rory before, and they got on well. He was a very pleasant person and was prepared to listen to other people. He agreed that it was possible that the boy had slept outdoors and had died accidentally of hypothermia, but he was open-minded and would wait to see what they found during the post-mortem.

When the examination commenced, the body of Aaron Wheeler lay out on the slab. Paul was thinking that however many times he saw this, there was something fundamentally wrong for young children to die so young, before their time. From past experience both Sue and Paul took the precaution of bringing along extra-strong mints, to help mitigate against the overwhelming smells pervading the mortuary.

Rory started with an external examination of the body, and he immediately looked surprised. "This is interesting, there are ligature marks around the neck."

"You mean he was strangled?" asked Sue.

"Unlikely, although the marks are clear and fresh, the injuries would not have been enough to cause death. But something was recently tied around his neck which then chafed the skin."

The post-mortem continued, Rory carefully dissecting and examining the body and its organs. Paul continued to reflect that it was the saddest thing, to see a child's body in the mortuary. There was so much more for him to do with his life, so much that he would now never be able to do. Somehow, for some reason, Aaron's future was stolen from him; Paul was determined to find out why.

Rory was thinking and talking through his thoughts, "Well, I can't quite rule out hypothermia but some of the classic signs are not present."

"What signs?" said Sue.

"This boy was fully dressed. Very often, in fact about fifty percent of hypothermia cases, victims will undress. We're not completely sure why it happens. Another feature of hypothermia is that victims will burrow down. This wasn't the case here, though."

"Why not, he was in a hole?" asked Sue.

"His nails. His nails are clean and unbroken. There is no mud on his hands at all, so someone else dug that hole and covered him over. Also, I understand it was quite mild, about ten degrees centigrade last night, so not so cold as to lower his core temperature dangerously."

"So, what killed him?" said Paul.

"I'm not sure, I need to send samples off for testing, but an overdose might be a possibility."

"What makes you think that?"

"He'd vomited and defecated over himself, which might be an indicator. Although the vomit and faeces are only on his body and under his clothing, so he must have got dressed after this happened."

"Overdose of what?" asked Sue.

Rory thought a while, "I don't want to speculate, we'll have to wait for the toxicology results…there are a few more things of significance: there is quite a bit of anal trauma present, in short, this little chap has been seriously buggered recently. Oh, that and the buttons on his shirt were misaligned and his underpants were inside out."

"Why after he died?"

"Well, because the vomit and faeces I found was inside but nothing outside his clothing."

Chapter 7

Capricorn and Pisces waited impatiently in the flat for Finn to arrive. It was just gone seven p.m. and they were trying to be patient but were both tense. They jumped when the doorbell rang. Pisces got up quickly, opened the door and ushered Finn inside.

Capricorn immediately grabbed Finn by the arm and squeezed hard. Finn winced but said nothing. Capricorn squeezed again, "I wanted to make sure that we understood each other. Your little friend is dead; it happens, you just make sure that you keep your mouth shut."

"I won't say anything…" started Finn.

"Damn right you won't, or you'll be sorry. Do not misunderstand me, I will do you in, if you say a *word*, and no one will care. You know I can control what the police do, they're not even investigating your friend's death."

Finn was suitably cowed and stood there looking at his feet. The fact that he enjoyed the power of being associated with these people made it frightening nonetheless. Finn knew what these people were capable of.

The Zodiac Club was made up of six men, all with an interest in young boys. The club was so called because the club members all referred to themselves as the name of a star sign. It was Finn's job to get young boys for the party, and sometimes take part himself. Finn knew that all the club members were influential, although Finn didn't know their real names, just their used code names. Capricorn was the leader and was something to do with the police. Pisces owned the fish-and-chip shop, and, of course, he knew Taurus who ran Manningsbrook children's home. There were also Aries, Libra and Scorpio but he didn't know much about them, except that Libra was something to do with the town council.

Taurus had introduced Finn to the club two years ago, and Finn had proven himself worthy, easily taking advantage of the young, vulnerable boys who came through the home's doors.

Finn knew he had to comply for fear of his life, but he wanted to be part of the club as well. It all went wrong with Aaron, though. It was Aaron's first time and he was scared. He was willing to try because of the rewards on offer but was still nervous. Finn told him that he could get cash, a mobile phone, trainers; whatever he wanted. All he had to do was go along with Finn and see what it was like. Finn knew that once he started there was no going back.

The parties were good because they always started with vodka, but the boys would then be given Rohypnol. Finn didn't like it; the Rohypnol made him woozy and do things he might otherwise be reluctant to do. Afterwards he'd sleep and have gaps in his memory. Aaron drank the glass of vodka but didn't like it. He took the Rohypnol and immediately looked out of it.

They stripped him, then put a dog collar and lead on him. They walked him around on all fours like a skinny, shaking puppy, all the while taking photos with good quality 35mm cameras. Libra, Scorpio and Pisces were the only three present and were loving the entertainment. The boy was ideal, Finn had outdone himself, as the boy was small thin and best of all, young. All three were agreed that seven was a good age to start a boy's education.

The boy's eyes were blank and lifeless as they paraded him to his best advantage. Libra then walked him into the grubby bedroom, furnished only with a single bed with a soiled duvet. Libra closed the door behind him and came out again five minutes later with a satisfied smirk on his face.

Pisces went next and was a bit longer but as he walked him out of the bedroom, suddenly the boy just keeled over onto his back. Aaron heaved and shook as he threw up the contents of his stomach and emptied his bowels onto the filthy carpet. Very soon, far from being the gorgeous young thing he used to be, the boy now looked like carnage and smelled of ordure.

Scorpio reacted first. He turned Aaron onto his side because he was choking on the blood and vomit spewing from his mouth. This did little to alleviate Aaron's problem, because he was still choking.

"Who can do CPR?" said Scorpio.

"Mouth to mouth, are you mad? Look at that mess, no way!" said Libra.

They all looked at each other, Libra's comment had pushed them into inaction. Finn was completely frozen; he was wide-eyed and shaking with fear. They all watched as Aaron continued to convulse until he finally stopped several minutes later. For Finn it was like a horror show; Aaron's blank eyes were wide open, staring accusingly at the group.

"Is he dead?" asked Scorpio.

"Well, he's not dancing, is he?" said Libra with heavy sarcasm, "Of course he's dead!" Libra switched into efficiency mode, becoming decisive. "We need to clean this mess up, and quick. We must get rid of the body; we can't have it linked to any of us. Finn get that dog collar off and get his clothes back on."

Finn looked up startled, "I… I can't!" he stammered.

Libra slapped him hard across the face, "You do it, or you join him."

Finn's eyes welled up, but he nodded, mutely, then carefully removed the collar. Finn struggled hard to get him dressed; he came to understand the meaning of the phrase "dead weight".

"Pisces, is your van round the back?" continued Libra.

"Yes."

"OK, let's find something to wrap the body in then go and dump it. I know of a quiet, out of the way place where we can hide it," said Libra, now fully in charge. "I'll call Taurus to create a cover story for him being out. He can say he ran off to sleep rough for the night. We'll need to tell Capricorn; he won't be happy, though. We can do this together, but we need to stay calm and stay focused."

The three men, with a shaken Finn looking on, wrapped the body in an old bed sheet. It was starting to get dark, so they hoped that they could sneak out unnoticed.

Libra said to Finn, in a kindlier tone now, "Come on, you should get home. You've had a terrible shock. Speak to Taurus, you'll be OK if you don't tell anyone about this. Also, start thinking about a replacement."

"What?" said Finn.

"You know our deal; you need to find a replacement for Aaron."

Finn was still in shock from all that had happened so just nodded dumbly and started to walk out.

"Good boy," said Libra with a stony expression.

For all his bravado Finn was only thirteen and was still a child. Finn had been a good soldier for the club but would still need watching. Thankfully, Taurus was perfectly positioned to monitor him.

The club members carried the sheet-covered body down to the dark car park at the rear of the flats. The iron stairway was noisy and the three had to choke down screams as the security lights blazed on as they reached the bottom. The three froze as if picked up by a spotlight. They almost expected to hear someone shout 'stop'! But no one did. They loaded the body into the rear of the 2002 model, white Ford Escort van.

Aaron's body felt unexpectedly bulky and cumbersome, it was difficult to load without just throwing the body in. They seemed to come to a realisation at the same time that there was little point in delicacy, so on the count of three they heaved the body into the back, then drove off to the marina area. They stopped in a quiet car park which was remote but gave access to an overgrown pathway at the rear. In the dark it looked like the perfect place to conceal a body.

All three had torches, Pisces and Scorpio carried the body with Libra leading the way. They turned right onto the pathway, their torches flicking around, creating eerie shapes in the adjacent woodland. They walked a while then Libra announced, “This is far enough.” He pointed into a clearing in the thick undergrowth. “In there, I don’t think anyone comes down this way.”

It was at that point that they realised that they had nothing to dig with. After a few recriminations Pisces volunteered to go back to the van and get something. When he returned, he had a small garden trowel in his hand.

“Is that all you’ve got? OK, get digging.” said Libra.

Pisces protested, “Why me?”

“Do you expect *me* to dig?”

“No, I’ll do it,” Pisces conceded, knowing his place in the hierarchy.

The power struggle quickly ended and normal service was resumed. Pisces managed to dig down a few feet and no further. Libra decided that would be enough, so they unwrapped the body from the sheet and placed it feet first into the hole. After they had covered the body with soil, branches and leaves, it now looked indistinguishable from the surrounding area.

Thinking that would be good enough they were all happy to go back to the van. As they climbed into the van, the sense of relief they all felt was enormous; they'd gotten away without being seen.

Pisces started the engine but as he was about to drive off, suddenly an old Vauxhall Corsa pulled into the car park at some speed. Seeing the van, it quickly turned around and left; there were two occupants. Obviously, they were a courting couple looking for privacy, but what did they see?

Chapter 8

"Well, it looks like there is still an investigation despite your attempt to stop it." Aries was scathing and Capricorn looked uncomfortable.

"Look I tried, there is only so much I can do," Capricorn muttered.

The Zodiac Club members were all meeting together in the flat to discuss the death of Aaron Wheeler. Finn wasn't there, having come earlier to receive a lecture from Capricorn. In any case Finn wasn't a member of the club, he was an asset, a soldier; he was useful but expendable. The club had been formed nearly ten years ago by founding members Capricorn and Aries. They had met each other originally by networking through a "Minor Attracted Adult" website based in America. The website tries to justify paedophilia and encourages networking between adults attracted to children. They organise meetings and conventions all over the world and had a decidedly evangelical approach to paedophilia. When they met, Capricorn and Aries were pleased and amazed to learn that they lived so close to each other and stayed connected on the dark web, sharing images of mutual interest.

Their friendship grew as did their ambitions to create the club. They met others through paedophile forums as time moved on and they now numbered six. They were mostly influential men in a small area, able to pursue their common interest. Two of their most useful members were Taurus, who ran the local children's home and Pisces who gave them the flat for their meetings. Like many other paedophiles, they were convinced that it was right to have sex with children. They believed that children were sexualised creatures who benefitted from the sexual interaction with their elders.

Taurus would take in vulnerable young boys, whom he carefully groomed and controlled. He used other boys like Finn to recruit as well; these boys were also useful to instil fear and to intimidate younger children. He had managed to procure dozens of boys in this way, offering them rewards and special treatment in the home. If anyone played up, they were moved on with a black mark against their name. Sometimes one of them would try to say what was happening, but who would believe them? Once one of the boys became so problematic they had to make him disappear. But again, no one really cared, these were troublesome kids always prone to running off and were not missed.

Aries then spoke up quietly, but authoritatively, "May I suggest that we all protect ourselves by keeping our heads down for a couple of weeks?"

Capricorn responded, "I agree, no Zodiac Club meetings for two weeks. But we need to keep going, we can't just fall apart. I spoke to Finn earlier, he seems OK but will need watching, he's a potential weak link."

Taurus chipped in, "I'll watch out for him, he'll be no trouble, and if he is… well…"

"What can we do about the investigation, if it's going ahead, as it seems to be?" asked Scorpio.

"I can find out what's happening with the investigation, I'll alert you if there is any risk to us," said Capricorn.

"What do you mean 'us'?! I wasn't even there!" complained Aries belligerently, in his usual pompous fashion.

Capricorn looked sternly at Aries until he saw his resolve weaken, then said calmly, "Neither was I, but we're all in this together."

Taurus nodded, "I agree, if one of us gets caught we're all in trouble. Don't forget, we got away with it once, we'll do it again, we've just got to keep it together."

The six looked at each other, waiting for someone to speak first. No one spoke but everyone was thinking about the consequences of being caught. They all had a lot to lose but no one had any thoughts of stopping the club. After all this wasn't the first time that the club had had to get rid of a problem.

Taurus was thinking of three years ago when there were only four members of the Zodiac Club; Aries (a vicar) and Scorpio (a businessman) hadn't yet joined them. Finn hadn't yet arrived on the scene, but Taurus had found a young boy called Jamie Simpson. He'd arrived at the children's home; twelve years old, tattoos on his face and arms, with an attitude that the whole world was out to get him. His mother was a heroin addict, a shoplifter and a prostitute, so Jamie didn't have a great role model to start with. He came to Manningsbrook because his mother had been given a custodial sentence and he had nowhere else to go, nor anyone willing to look after him.

When he was delivered by the social worker to the home, he was full of anger and hatred and quickly got into bother. What Taurus saw in Jamie, though, was a troubled soul with an angelic face. Taurus genuinely cared for the children in his care and took Jamie under his wing. For the first time, Jamie experienced what it was like to have someone take an interest in his welfare. They quickly formed a bond; although Jamie was wary, Rogers treated him with relentless fairness and kindness, even when he was having to challenge some misbehaviour or other.

For the first time in his life Jamie had found an adult he could trust. At this point Taurus introduced Jamie to the Zodiac Club. To say it went badly would be an understatement. Jamie was in the flat with Taurus, Capricorn and Aries and it had started well. He happily drank the vodka, and when his third drink was spiked with Rohypnol, he readily took his shirt off and danced with the men. It all went blurry from there and when he woke the following morning, he knew something had been done to him. Jamie felt betrayed and violated. In fact, he felt worse than he had ever felt before, in what he thought of as his shitty little life. At least before with his mum he had no expectations of her. All the crap he previously suffered was what he expected. With Rogers he thought that he had someone who cared for him and that Rogers had his best interests at heart. The pain of the disappointment was unbearable, and his anger extreme.

On realising what must have happened to him, Jamie started by crying for the first time in years but after a few minutes he stopped, then stormed into the office to confront Rogers.

With his back to the door Rogers didn't see Jamie coming, so was startled when he barged in shouting, "The Zodiac Club! What did you all do to me?"

Taken aback, Rogers stuttered, "N… n… nothing, keep quiet people will hear."

"Let them hear; I don't care, I know what you did, I just want to hear you say it."

Realising that one of the staff, Luke, was heading towards the office, Rogers stood up and closed the door. He whispered fiercely to Jamie, "Look, come with me, let's talk about it."

There was a knock on the door. Rogers didn't open the door but called out, "It's OK Luke, I'm handling this, everything is under control."

Jamie then spoke, "Look, you Zodiac Club bastards are going to pay for what you've done. If you don't pay me what I want, I'll go to the law."

"How much do you want?"

"I'll think about it. I'll let you know, but it will be a lot."

"No problem, we can sort this out. You don't want to do anything silly."

Jamie stormed off towards his room and Rogers was left staring at Luke who was standing in the hall outside the office.

Chapter 9

DI Sue Taylor was sat in her office with DCI Steve Jones, looking over the toxicology report from the pathologist for Aaron Wheeler.

"Rohypnol; it was date rape, then?" said Steve.

"Looks likely that he was stupefied with the drug probably for sex, we were lucky to find it, Rohypnol doesn't stay in the body very long," said Sue.

"There's a high level of alcohol as well."

Sue, who had read the report earlier nodded, "Yes, that's the thing. You mix alcohol with Rohypnol and it can be extremely dangerous."

Steve nodded his agreement and Sue continued, "Combined with the evidence of sexual abuse, even Irvine must now see it's a murder investigation."

Steve looked grim, "I agree, we'll write the policy book together outlining all our thoughts on this. We'll get an enquiry room started here at Leeston; I'll speak to HQ."

"HQ, you mean Irvine?"

"Who else, he is our boss, after all, I know you don't like him."

"It's not just that I don't like him. I don't trust him either."

As he was speaking, the local uniformed inspector, Jon Thorne, poked his head through the doorway, "Sorry to interrupt folks, but can you tell me what's happening with the found body?"

Sue thought that Jon was pleasant and affable enough. He'd been at Leeston forever and headed the uniformed branch of the police there. He was a steady hand but not particularly dynamic. Sue thought he always seemed a little stiff and uncomfortable with her. Maybe he wasn't confident around women, she mused.

Sue was happy to talk to him, "Hi Jon, that's great timing. Yes, we've got the pathologist's report back: we're definitely looking at murder."

Inspector Thorne's face stiffened, "Oh, dear, in that case is there anything I can do?"

"We may need some staff if possible, but can I let you know, we're just getting started?"

"Of course, if you need anything let me know. I've got a community meeting this evening, but you can always get hold of me by phone."

Sue called her thanks as Jon Thorne marched off.

"Nice guy," said Sue.

She picked up the phone and spoke to Paul Smith, "Paul, I've got the toxicology report, we're definitely looking at a murder."

"No real surprise there then!" said Paul.

"We need to get our skates on. We're now behind the curve so we can't waste time. I want you to take a team to

Manningsbrook Children's home; speak to the manager, staff and children — get as much background information as possible. While you're there we need to search the home for clues; in particular, his room and belongings. Get someone to do a CCTV review of the areas round the home and where the body was deposited, we need to recover any possible footage. There must be something with him on." Sue reeled off a series of urgent actions which she wanted completed as a priority.

"Is that all?" asked Paul.

"For now," said Sue, "I'll find more for you to do, don't worry."

Paul thought about responding but instead said, "In that case I'd best get going then, I'll keep you posted."

Sue and Steve spent the next few hours getting the investigation up and running, getting staff in place and identifying lines of enquiry.

"We have a suspect!" Sally, the intelligence analyst, said breathlessly to Sue as she rushed into the squad room. Sally was always the first one Sue asked to start researching information sources. As usual Sally came up trumps.

"Great news," Sue smiled, "who is it?"

"His father, or in fact, his stepfather, a man called John Gulliver." Sally was reading a document. "I have Aaron's child protection file here. John Gulliver is a very nasty man with a long string of violent convictions. Aaron's mum was given a choice, either leave John Gulliver or lose her son."

"I guess she chose Gulliver?"

"Yes, but at the last meeting with the social worker Gulliver said, that if Aaron went into care he might as well be dead and threatened to track him down and kill him."

"That's awful."

"That's the type of man he is. He has convictions for assaulting his own children from former partners as well."

"OK, get me DS Smith, we need to arrest Gulliver as soon as we can."

Paul Smith came into her office ten minutes later. "I've spoken to Sally, he sounds like a nasty guy, I'll get him in."

"Take care though, Paul. Go with a firearms team; he's got warning markers on the computer for using guns."

An hour later Paul sat in the briefing room with the firearms team going over the information and the tactics they would use. Paul was to go to a magistrate to get a warrant to enter the house. The firearms team would break in at four a.m. and secure Gulliver before he had a chance to wake up.

The magistrate had no difficulty granting a warrant, so Paul managed to go home for a short while to change and grab a couple of hours sleep before the alarm went off. At one a.m. he woke up, disorientated, until he remembered why he had been so rudely disturbed. He immediately got up, dressed and headed to work, buzzing with excitement.

Paul met up with the firearms team at the rendezvous point near to Lindmouth, as Gulliver lived near there. After a quick check to make sure everything was in place they drove off in convoy. They covered the front and rear of the two-bedroomed terraced council house. The Tactical Firearms Team officers were all dressed in black, military style combat clothing, with masks and helmets. When they were in position, the rear team managed to remove the patio door without making a sound. They crept soundlessly through the kitchen to the hallway, checking the lounge on the way past, then opened the front door to let the rest of the team in.

The team spread out as the operational commander led them upstairs. Entering the main bedroom, they could make out a massive bulk on the bed next to a smaller shape. There was heavy snoring coming from the bed which was a good sign. The lead officer moved close to the snoring hulk, "Wakey, wakey sleepy-head."

In a sudden move, Gulliver flew out of bed with a roar, grabbing at the officer and throwing him to the floor. Someone turned on a light to better see the shouting, swearing and fighting that ensued. The TFT officers were all fit and well trained but Gulliver was big and nasty and an experienced street fighter. There was a huge melee as Gulliver lashed out viciously. Eventually he was overcome and restrained but not before one inexperienced officer had managed to accidentally deploy his taser to his colleague's leg in the confusion, to much subsequent hilarity in those officers not affected. To add to the fun, the woman in the bed, who was Aaron's mum, Alice Wheeler, was shouting and swearing at the police and was punching anyone who came near her, until she could be restrained.

Once he was overcome, cuffed and thrown in the van, Gulliver had finally calmed down, but not before causing some damage. Almost all of the officers were nursing minor cuts and bruises, but they were all on a high having managed to get Gulliver into police custody.

Chapter 10

Taurus clearly remembered the night that they met Jamie at the flat for the second time. It was a stormy night, and everyone got wet as they had made their separate ways to the flat.

Taurus had convinced Jamie to meet the Zodiac Club to discuss how they could resolve his grievance against them. For his part, Jamie wanted payback for what he thought had been done to him. He had no clear memory of that Zodiac party, but just knew that he had been raped by these men. He was convinced that something had happened because of the drugs. And there were physical signs: his groin was sore, and he had bled from his arse. He knew that this sort of thing went on but couldn't believe that it had happened to him.

The living room was gloomy, lit only by the bare lightbulb hanging limply in the middle of the room. They sat on the old, brown velour sofas. Jamie sat on his own while Capricorn, Aries and Taurus sat together. The heating was on and the flat was too hot, the dampness from the rain made Jamie feel uncomfortable.

Jamie started, "I know what you are, and I know what you did to me."

Capricorn took the lead. Smiling warmly, he said, "What do you know?"

"I know you're all paedos, you got me drunk then bummed me."

Capricorn remained calm and the rest stayed silent, "So what do you want to do about it?"

This took Jamie by surprise, he'd expected arguments or denials, but it wasn't like that. Jamie thought for a moment, "I want some money, if you don't give me money I'll go to the law."

Capricorn was a model of equanimity, "How much would you like?"

Jamie was clearly unprepared because he nervously hesitated, then said, "A thousand pounds, you have to give me a thousand pounds."

"Very reasonable," said Capricorn.

Taurus remained silent but Aries looked outraged, "Now look here—"

Capricorn stood up, interrupting Aries. "Aries, our young friend has been kind enough to come and see us rather than go to the police, we should at least give him the courtesy of hearing him out."

As he spoke, Capricorn had moved over to stand next to where Jamie was sitting, as if in solidarity with him.

Emboldened Jamie said, "That's right; if you pay me, I'll forget it ever happened."

Capricorn continued, relaxed with his hands in his pockets, "The only problem is that what you're talking about is blackmail, which is against the law. We can't break the law, can we?"

"If you don't pay, I'll tell the police."

Capricorn laughed at that, "I *am* the police, you fool." He paused to see the reaction, then continued more threateningly, "How can we trust that you won't keep blackmailing us, that you won't keep asking for more? Sorry we can't go down that route, we will not be blackmailed by a little scumbag like you."

Jamie was confused by the unexpected turn of events, but chose anger as a response, "If you're really a copper, the price has just doubled to two thousand."

Capricorn suddenly snapped, he pulled a heavy cosh out of his pocket, then hit Jamie repeatedly over the head. Jamie tried to defend himself but was trapped in the comfortable sofa which held him nicely in place to be hit. Jamie lashed out with his arms and legs, but Capricorn kept hitting him wherever he could. After ten seconds the attack stopped, Capricorn breathing heavily, Jamie lying unconscious, barely breathing. After a while he stopped breathing and just lay lifeless, his eyes wide in what looked like comic surprise.

Taurus spoke mildly, "A little excessive, don't you think?"

Aries then found his voice; he was in shock, "*Excessive?* Are you both mad? Having two puddings is excessive… that was sheer bloody murder!"

Capricorn was cool, "There was no choice, he would have bled us dry, then betrayed us anyway."

"You planned this!" accused Aries.

"I thought it was a possibility that things might get rough, so I prepared for this eventuality."

Taurus added his thoughts, "Well I think you had to make a call, and it was the right one. He was a proper little shit; we could never have trusted him."

The three discussed what to do next; they had to get rid of Jamie's body. Capricorn had brought along a sleeping bag, having already thought this through. They put the corpse in the sleeping bag then called Pisces to come and clean the flat which was a bloody mess, looking like the aftermath of a battle from the middle ages.

When it was dark enough, they drove down to the waterside near to the marina. Two of them carried the body along a little used path. By a strange coincidence they passed the very spot where Aaron Wheeler would be buried three years later. They loaded the sleeping bag with rocks then, taking a small boat, rowed out to a sufficient depth before dropping the body over the side. It sank swiftly in a swirl of bubbles. They waited a while in case the body resurfaced. When it hadn't, satisfied with their work, they rowed ashore.

Jamie was reported missing the following day; no one was really surprised; he'd never been happy at the home. The missing persons police report suggested that he must have headed home to link up with his old friends. Cursory police enquiries were initiated to try to trace him, but after a while the file was closed and he was never heard of again.

Chapter 11

It was late afternoon and DS Paul Smith was monitoring the interview of John Gulliver. Two of his best interviewers were talking to the monolith before them. He might as well have been a block of stone because he didn't even bother to say, "no comment"; instead, Gulliver just stared at them with loathing. He had demanded a solicitor on his arrival, who was present in the interview. The solicitor said nothing for forty-five minutes when the frustrated interviewers had exhausted their list of questions covering his past, his involvement with Aaron and his mum, and his movements on the night of Aaron's death. At this point the solicitor pushed across a sheet of paper with the words 'Strings Nightclub' and 'Birmingham City Hospital' scrawled across it.

One of the interviewers picked the paper up. "What's this?"

"Where my client was the night the boy died. He got into a fight with bouncers in a nightclub, then spent the rest of the night in A & E. It's all verifiable."

"Forgive me if we don't just take your word for that."

Gulliver flared up, fists clenched, a vein pulsing on his enormous head, "Fuck this, I'm getting out of here."

Gulliver stood up in the tiny interview room and started to walk out. Nervous and scared, one of the interviewers pressed the panic button on the wall and within seconds a stream of officers flooded the room looking for a fight. Gulliver, despite his size and strength, was forced to the ground and roughly handcuffed.

The solicitor had backed into a corner and was shaking, as white as a ghost. "I… I'm not sure that was necessary."

"We'll look into the alibi then let you know," said Paul Smith, who had also rushed in when the alarm went.

Paul immediately despatched two of his team to check the nightclub and hospital records as well as any CCTV. He knew Sue would want this done asap.

Having made sure that Gulliver was bedded down for the night, Paul turned his attention to the children's home. Interviewing staff and children at Manningsbrook proved harder than Paul Smith had thought. DC Jo James and a couple of other DCs came along to help. They decided to search the home first, but it was a lot larger than they had anticipated. Paul decided to concentrate on Aaron's room. The room was high-ceilinged and had three beds in it. There were posters covering much of the walls and it looked like any boy's bedroom with things scattered everywhere.

Aaron had his own bed, bedside cabinet and two drawers in the cabinet. He had few clothes and fewer possessions. Paul was saddened to think how little Aaron had and how brutally it had been snatched away from him.

They found nothing of significance in the room other than an old photograph of a man, woman and a boy in a play park. Presumably, this was Aaron with his parents; Paul wondered what had happened to bring him to Manningsbrook. The kids at the home so often had incredibly sad stories. A lot of them had behavioural problems which was understandable when you knew their backgrounds.

Searching the common areas of the care home yielded even less. Aaron had made no imprint on the home, it was as though he'd never been there, perhaps he hadn't been there long enough. Interviewing the children was fruitless, it seemed that none of them knew him well, and none of them was his friend. Paul Smith and Jo James interviewed Finn Oliver, who was the oldest resident and seemed to assume a leadership role with the other children.

Paul Smith had an odd feeling about Finn, who was surly and difficult. "Tell me what you know of Aaron," said Paul.

"Nothing," mumbled Finn, eyes averted.

"Describe him for me."

"What do you mean?"

"What was he like?"

"Don't know… quiet?"

"What do you mean?"

"Well I never talked to him, but he didn't say much."

Paul hesitated and looked at Jo. Jo said, "We have witnesses who say you were talking to him the day he went missing."

"What witnesses? That's not possible… they're lying. I may have said hello sometimes, but we never talked."

Ignoring Finn's previous answer, Jo continued, "Jade said she heard you mention something called the Zodiac Club."

"That's bollocks, I already told Luke she is a liar."

"What is the Zodiac Club?" asked Jo.

Finn hesitated for a fraction of a second. "No idea, never heard of it, that means nothing to me."

"Do you know what happened to Aaron?"

Again, a micro-hesitation, "No idea. Can I go now?"

After Finn had left, Paul and Jo looked at each other, then almost simultaneously said, "I don't trust him."

They looked each other in the eye, laughed and suddenly a connection was made between them. Jo had always had a soft spot for Paul, but nothing was ever said. Paul was diffident around women, and never thought that someone like Jo would be interested in him anyway. This felt like a seismic shift in their relationship and Paul inwardly vowed to try to allow things to develop between them if the chance arose.

Neither of them believed everything Finn had told them, but they had no real idea what it was he was lying about. They also knew that just because he was lying, it didn't mean that he was involved in Aaron's death. People had a lot of different motivations to lie, it wasn't always to cover up a crime.

The other children were equally uncommunicative, but that could just mean that they didn't know anything. Their dilemma was that all the police officers had a strong impression that the residents were hiding something... what though?

To make matters worse there were inconsistencies in what the staff were telling them. The manager, Alan, described Aaron as streetwise and prone to going missing whereas the other staff members described him as shy and quiet and not one to disappear. Paul decided to interview the manager again and get Jo to speak to Luke and Sophie to see why there were differences in their stories.

Paul found Alan in his office. "Mr Rogers, can I please clear something up?"

"Of course."

"We have a discrepancy between you and your staff about whether Aaron had gone missing before."

Alan Rogers smiled, "Well technically he hadn't been missing because he'd never been reported. It's just that a few times he had wandered off on his own. It probably hasn't happened when the others were on duty. I wouldn't say they are lying, exactly."

Paul thought a moment, "Well that does make sense. Can I see the records of these missing episodes?"

"Why?"

"Just crossing the Ts."

Rogers looked remorseful, "Guilty as charged."

"Sorry?"

"Look I consider myself to be a good care home manager and I feel like I do my best for the kids. Alas, in truth I am also a terrible administrator, my file keeping is not what it should be. In short, I have no records of Aaron going missing," said Rogers, apologetically.

"So how do you know he goes off, and how often?" asked Paul.

"Because this is my care home and I know everything that goes on here."

As they were driving back to the station, Jo and Paul compared notes on their respective interviews. They found it confusing that the manager had such a different view of Aaron from Luke and Sophie. Did it matter anyway? It just felt like a loose end, and Paul didn't like loose ends. He was thinking that the trip to the children's home hadn't been very productive, but who knew how it would all fit into the jigsaw as they put the pieces together?

As they were pulling into the station car park, Jo said something completely unexpected, "So Paul, when are you going to ask me out?"

Paul blushed, then stammered, "I… I… do you want me to?"

Jo replied, "You're going to have to eventually, that is if you want to?"

Paul grew in confidence, "Well, do you want to?"

Jo laughed, "You're a romantic, aren't you?"

"Not really, but do you want to go out?"

"I'd love to," said Jo, they then fell into silence.

That wasn't awkward at all, she thought, *but at least we're over that hurdle, let's hope that we can sort out a date soon.* But for now, they had a murder to investigate.

As Paul and Jo briefed DI Sue Taylor and DCI Steve Jones, they expressed their unease about the information they'd managed to get or, in truth, failed to get. They felt that there were a number of inconsistencies but did not know whether anyone was lying, and who it might be if anyone were. They both thought that the Finn boy was untrustworthy and seemed to control the rest of the children. But did that mean anything sinister?

Another resident, Jade, had told them that she'd heard Aaron talking to Finn about something called the Zodiac Club on the day he went missing. They'd asked around but no one seemed to know what or where the club was, and Finn denied the conversation completely. So, given the circumstances, they weren't a lot further forward, not knowing who to believe.

Sue was most interested in the Zodiac Club and raised a high priority action to identify its location and purpose. Someone must know something about it if it existed at all.

Chapter 12

"Alan, why did you tell the police that Aaron had gone missing before?" Luke was in the office looking puzzled.

"Because he had… I'm surprised you didn't know that. I knew him better than you, he was pretty headstrong," said Alan.

Luke was taken aback, "What? Are we talking about the same boy? He was quiet and nervous."

"I think that says a lot about you. You don't connect with the children; that's your weakness. I'm sorry Luke, it's no good, I'll have to let you go."

Luke was shocked, he hadn't expected this when he'd decided to confront Alan, "Why?"

Alan was solemn, "Luke, I think we both know it's not been working out for a while now."

"What do you mean? You never said anything!" Luke was amazed.

"Let's not make this difficult, I'll give you a good reference, but you need to leave now. Otherwise, if you make a fuss, you'll leave with no reference."

Luke was quiet and gave in easily, "OK, I'll leave, but I really don't understand why."

"Off you go then, I'll pay you to the end of the month as a show of goodwill."

"Thanks Alan."

Luke shuffled out of the office, shell-shocked. He loved the job, he thought he was secure, having been there for several years. He never realised that there were problems.

When Luke had left, Alan telephoned Capricorn, "You'll be pleased to know that I've tied up another loose end."

Capricorn was curious, "Oh, yes?"

"Yes, I've just sacked one of my care workers, Luke."

"Why?"

"Well he was around when we got rid of Jamie and if he puts two and two together, he might connect that to Aaron. Also, he was challenging my statement that Aaron had gone missing before. I didn't want that point of view to gain momentum."

"OK then, let me know if it gets problematic; will he keep quiet now?"

"He's weak, he'll not cause a fuss," said Alan confidently.

Alan was a bully towards his staff by nature and couldn't see how Luke would have the nerve to try to take this any further. He'd have to talk to Sophie to make sure that she was on his side. He leaned back in his chair, closed his eyes and breathed deeply. He tried to settle his mind by listening to the comings and goings of the house. The familiar and comforting noises were as soothing as a balm to him. He loved this house and loved many of the children in his care. Alan could see no contradiction between his love for the children and the harm he caused.

Chapter 13

DS Paul Smith had plucked up the courage to invite Jo out that coming evening, providing they had no other urgent actions to complete. Paul hoped they'd get the chance to go out together, but it all depended on how the enquiry, now called Operation Mill, went. Jo had suggested a local pub that she knew which served good food. Just as they had arranged their date, Paul got a call from the team in Birmingham.

The detective sounded forlorn and frustrated, "Sorry, Sarge, Gulliver's got a cast-iron alibi. He had started a fight with some bouncers inside the nightclub entrance. We're not sure why it started, but he made a good fist of it, all caught on camera."

"Are you sure it's him?" Paul said, clutching at straws.

"You can't mistake him. Anyway, he got a nasty cut during the fight and was taken to A&E by ambulance. He checked in at two a.m. and was seen at six a.m. He's on CCTV all the time."

"So, he was in Birmingham when Aaron was killed. Damn it. Isn't that a convenient coincidence, do you think?"

"Maybe, but it all looks pukka, Sarge; he was here on a stag night, but he got pissed and for some reason took on the bouncers but lost. It was a close-run thing, though, he looks like a nasty bastard."

Paul was deflated, "You're right but he's probably not our murderer. Well, we can only follow the evidence, thanks for the update though."

The squad was now well-resourced since the press had picked up on the story. Owing to the now high-profile nature of the murder enquiry, a lot of brass were interested. There are few things more emotive than the murder of a child, even more so where sexual abuse was suspected. DCS Scotty Irvine quickly changed his previous tune when the Chief Constable called him to stress the priority of the investigation. Unusually for Irvine, he couldn't be more helpful, immediately sending detectives to assist. Paul was running the outside enquiry team and his workload was led by how many lines of enquiry were generated, and what information came into the intelligence team.

DCI Jones had held a press conference, appealing for witnesses or anyone with information to come forward. Steve Jones was particularly good at this, and when he was on the local six p.m. news, he came across as professional, intelligent and articulate. Press appeals could uncover excellent lines of enquiry and would often prompt people to call in with information they hadn't realised was useful.

The house-to-house enquiries had started, and the team were also collecting any CCTV en route from the home to the deposition site. Town centre CCTV was also being collected in case Aaron had been in town that afternoon.

The afternoon wore on and staff were busy chasing up the outstanding actions. Tasks were delegated to people on the enquiry to complete by way of written "actions", detailing what they needed to do.

Late in the day, one of the analysts, Sally, received a call from Luke Morgan. "Hello, can I speak to the investigators looking into Aaron Wheeler?"

"Of course, I can take a message and get someone to contact you. What is it regarding?"

"I work… *used* to work at the Manningsbrook children's home. I think I have some important information."

"About what?"

Luke hesitated a moment then spoke decisively, "I think I know where Aaron was going when he went missing."

Sally was immediately interested, "Can you tell me where?"

"It's something called the Zodiac Club. Jade heard Finn talking to Aaron about it, but Finn denied this. It didn't mean anything to me at the time, but I've just remembered that I'd heard the name before when another boy, Jamie Simpson, went missing some years ago. I'm wondering if there is some sort of connection."

"Well, that's especially useful information. We'll need a bit more detail but thank you for calling. I'll get a detective to see you as soon as possible."

By chance DS Paul Smith walked into the squad room as she put the phone down; Sally spotted him and called him over. She excitedly told him what Luke had said. Paul thought for a moment about getting someone else to go to see Luke so that he could go on his date with Jo, but his curiosity got the better of him. It sounded like such a good lead, he had to follow it up himself.

Paul phoned Jo to say he would be delayed, and she quickly offered to go with him. Paul was delighted at this compromise and they arranged to meet. He hoped that they might still go out later, though. To prepare for the meeting, Jo researched the long-term missing persons' files for Jamie Simpson.

Jo was surprised to discover that the missing person's file for Jamie had disappeared from storage. All the other long-term missing persons' files were stored separately, but for some reason this one was not there. There was a skeletal electronic record which gave scant detail of the circumstances of his going missing and the fact that there had been an investigation. There was no mention of anything called the Zodiac Club. The investigation had been closed after just four weeks, with the unsubstantiated statement that "he must have returned to his former life". Without proof, this seemed like an extraordinary assumption and, unusually, the report had been signed off by DCS Irvine. Jo wondered why a Detective Chief

Superintendent had taken an interest in a local missing boy if there was not anything suspicious.

Walking along the station corridor, Jo spotted Inspector Jon Thorne, "Hello sir, you were here three years ago, weren't you?"

"Yes, why?"

"Do you remember a boy going missing from the children's home, Jamie Simpson?"

Jon Thorne frowned, "A lot of children go missing from the home."

"Yes, but this one was never found. He was heard to mention the Zodiac Club; do you know anything about it?"

Jon Thorne looked surprised, "No I don't remember the boy, and I've never heard of any Zodiac Club, some sort of youth club is it?"

"We don't know, that's what we're trying to find out. What do you know about the staff at the home?"

Jon Thorne considered a moment, "I know the manager Alan Rogers, excellent fellow, been there years."

"What about Luke Morgan?"

"I don't know him, really. I think he's a bit unreliable. I'm sure I heard that Alan had some trouble with him."

"Thanks sir, that's very helpful."

Jo and Paul met up and drove over to see Luke, who lived on the outskirts of Swinton. They discussed the evidence they had so far, including what Inspector Thorne had said about Luke. It was all very confusing; there was so much conflicting information, it was hard to know what was true. They hoped that maybe Luke could shed some light on it all. With all the confusion and contradictory information, Paul was starting to think that the problem might be the home itself.

They drove in an old unmarked police car, which was characterised by the smell of old take-aways and a proliferation of used food wrappers. The car was mechanically well maintained but internally was in an appalling state, and Jo turned her nose up in disgust. This was typical of the CID cars, which were merely used as workhorses.

After they'd exhausted their conversation about the case Paul said, "So, are you still OK for a drink tonight if we get away in time?"

"No."

Paul was disappointed, but couldn't think of anything to say; what had he done wrong?

Jo continued, "No, you'll have to take me to dinner instead, since you made me miss my tea."

Jo smiled and Paul laughed nervously, then said, "Of course, do you like Italian?"

It was nearly eight p.m. by the time they had left Luke's flat. He lived alone in a tiny purpose-built studio flat, a key worker flat, he told them. Luke was depressed and demoralised from having been sacked and because he had been drinking, he struggled to articulate what he was thinking. From Luke's ramblings they gleaned some interesting insights.

To start with Luke told them that Alan Rogers favoured Finn. Luke was of the opinion that Finn was entirely unreliable and very dodgy. Finn always seemed to have too much money, the latest iPhone and often had expensive trainers and clothes. When Luke challenged him about this, Alan came to Finn's defence, bollocking Luke for interfering.

Luke told them about what he knew about the Zodiac Club, which was not much. He talked about when Jamie Simpson disappeared. He remembered the occasion when Jamie and Alan were arguing in the office; he couldn't exactly hear what was being said but it sounded like Jamie was accusing Alan of something. Luke was also certain that he'd heard Jamie shout something about the Zodiac Club. Luke remembered that there was another boy, Sean Moroney, in the hallway at the time who must have heard as well. He had no idea what the argument was all about, but Jamie had disappeared shortly afterwards.

Luke was surprised that no one was interested in Jamie going missing. Normally people seemed more anxious when children go missing. Luke hadn't said anything to the police about the argument he'd overheard because Alan asked him not to. Alan made it clear in a threatening way that he should say nothing about it and Luke didn't have the confidence to defy him. Jamie and Sean were close friends but when he left, Sean's personality changed, and he became difficult and argumentative.

Luke continued, saying that the next time he'd heard of the Zodiac Club was when Jade said she'd heard Finn talking to Aaron about it. Luke was adamant that Aaron would not have gone missing of his own volition. He described Aaron as a timid, quiet boy who had never gone anywhere on his own; he had no idea why Alan should say differently.

Once again, they had more questions than answers and a number of contradictions. Paul and Jo drove back, their heads spinning with their own thoughts. But who were they to believe? Finn was entirely untrustworthy, they thought. But was Luke reliable or not; or was Alan Rogers misleading them? Paul would make sure that fast-track actions were raised to interview both Jamie Simpson and Sean Moroney about the past. However, Paul had a bad feeling that they would never be able to find Jamie.

Chapter 14

Finn was feeling the pressure; he had a tough exterior, but inside he was really a frightened child. He had been totally shocked by Aaron's death; he also felt guilty because he had persuaded Aaron to go along to the Zodiac Club. In fairness to himself, he had done it many times before with no trouble. How was he to know that Aaron couldn't take it? Alan had told him not to blame himself; in actual fact, he didn't blame himself, he blamed the Zodiac Club. They were the ones who plied boys with drink and drugs; they must have known that it could go wrong at some point.

Now Finn was in the position that he had to find someone else to go to the club. It wasn't that easy, but he had a method. First Finn had to befriend the boy; he'd give them cigarettes, money and drink; then get them to come along to the club. By that point they were good friends so getting them to come was easy enough. After they'd been, Finn needed to control them by blackmail and with threats of violence. All this took time and effort, and it was important to pick the right boy; no one could afford any of them going to the police. Mind you, if he were careful, it's unlikely that they'd go to the police, and if they did, they'd be unlikely to be believed. In any case, if all else failed, they had a man in the police who could make things go away. They'd told Finn the story of how they'd dealt with Jamie; this was as much to impress as to scare him. Finn was impressed, he liked power, he also liked the money and gifts, like his new iPhone.

Finn came from what you'd call humble beginnings, but not so bad and certainly not unusual. He'd had a mum and dad and two younger brothers; they weren't poor but not rich either. It started to change when his dad left; he didn't leave for any reason, other than he no longer wanted a family. He worked long hours, by choice, and didn't much engage with the children, always claiming tiredness from work. When even this became too onerous for him, he left. He didn't just leave, though, he moved abroad. He moved to a remote village in the Pyrenees near the border of Spain and France. He was gone, out of their lives, leaving his mum to try to raise three children on her own. Finn was nine when his dad left, and it hit him hardest. His behaviour deteriorated; he got himself excluded from school for fighting. What was worse though, was that he had a knife and threatened another boy with it. When a teacher came to break it up, he threatened the teacher too. After exclusion, he got in with a crowd, hanging around the local park. They drank and used drugs; life got out of hand.

Eventually, social services got involved and it was obvious that his mother could not cope with him. So, Finn was moved fifty miles away to Manningsbrook children's home. He'd been there about two years, which was unusual, but Alan could pull strings, and Finn caused no trouble, so everyone let it go.

Now Finn was confused, he didn't know if he should stay or try to leave. He had to find someone else for the club otherwise he could end up like Aaron and Jamie. No one currently at the home was suitable, but hopefully Alan could get someone soon to maybe replace Aaron. The truth was that there were always children needing a bed to sleep in, so there would be no problem with getting someone; it just needed to be the right someone.

Chapter 15

DS Paul Smith and DC Jo James finished briefing DI Taylor and DCI Jones and there was a pause as everyone marshalled their thoughts.

Steve Jones spoke first, “Whatever is going on, it looks like it has something to do with Manningsbrook Children’s Home.”

Sue nodded, “I agree but I think we have an opportunity we can exploit if we’re quick.”

“What do you mean?” asked Jo.

Paul, who was usually on Sue’s wavelength, replied, “I think she’s thinking of getting one of our own in.”

“Yes, I am, with Luke getting fired, we can try to get someone in undercover to take the job. What do you think, Steve?”

“It all seems to point to Manningsbrook, so if we can get someone in to find out what’s going on, I’m all for it.”

“They’ll need to know about social care to fit in,” Jo suggested.

“I know just the person, a young DC who works for me in covert operations who used to be a social worker,” said Steve, “I’ll get him on board straight away. I also know the head of children's services; I'll get that vacant job put aside for us."

"Sounds great," said Paul, "I'll write up all the paperwork for formal authorisation; it will take a small forest."

"I'll help," said Sue, "after all I'll be running the operation. It goes without saying, that no one is to speak of this."

"So, what in particular will our covert operative try to do?" queried Steve.

"I think Finn Oliver knows more than he is letting on; we'll get our man to befriend him and find out what he knows," Sue replied.

Jo chimed in, "And find out about the Zodiac Club."

"Yes, and check out that manager, Alan Rogers, is he trustworthy?"

"Let's not forget the other staff and children, they probably know something," suggested Paul.

The meeting quickly broke up after this.

"Jo seems pretty switched on," Steve remarked to Sue, as they walked away.

"Yes, she and Paul work well together," Sue said, with a knowing smile.

Arranging a covert operation meant a huge amount of work, not least of which was the paperwork to request permission, fulfilling the requirements of the Surveillance Commissioner. Sue and Paul sequestered themselves to start typing while Steve hit the phones. Steve was glad to hear that the head of children's services would be willing for them to put a covert officer in the home, though she took some persuading. Luckily, Steve knew her well as they'd worked together previously, but it still took all of his powers of persuasion to convince her.

The next call ensured his officer's availability. Finding an undercover officer with social care experience is not easy, so having someone "homegrown" was ideal. In fact, Harry Thomson was perfect, having been raised in care himself. His experience in care was mostly positive, and he did well as a care leaver, going to university and getting his degree. Harry had initially become a social worker to try to give something back. He left when he became frustrated at the lack of resources, and what he thought was his inability to make a lasting difference, so he decided to try policing instead.

Harry thrived in the police, finding that the discipline and the environment of working with teams of people suited him very well. Harry was twenty-eight but looked younger; he was perfect for working undercover in this role, looking more like a student social worker than a policeman.

Having worked on frontline policing for a couple of years, he moved onto the CID and then volunteered for covert operations. He was particularly adept at drug gang infiltration, so was intrigued when DCI Steve Jones came to him about this latest job.

Steve outlined the situation and said, "We think there is something wrong at Manningsbrook but we're not sure what. We need you to get information about whatever is going on; in particular, find out about the Zodiac Club and see what it is."

"OK," said Harry, "I guess I'll be incommunicado?"

"No, we'll have daily contact with you. DI Taylor will be your contact, she'll talk about how you keep in touch, and tell you about the extraction plan."

"OK, when do I start?"

"As soon as I can get authority to run the operation. Please remember these people may have committed murder already, so they could be desperate and dangerous."

"I'll try to remember."

Chapter 16

Having finally finished work for the evening, and agreed upon dinner, Paul Smith and Jo James settled on Giorgio's Italian restaurant in Leeston.

The restaurant was in a Tudor building over two floors and had a comfortable feeling. The interior was dark with heavy oak beams and low lighting. The oak tables with dark brown leather chairs were housed in a green painted, oak panelled room. A wrought iron spiral staircase dominated the middle of the room, leading to more seating upstairs. An enormous brick pizza oven stood at the far end of the restaurant and the pizzas were prepared and cooked in full view of the customers.

They had a nice, quiet table in a corner and the restaurant was fairly busy. The staff were efficient, courteous and attentive and the food amazing. Paul offered not to drink so that Jo could enjoy a couple of glasses of wine. Jo was touched by this thoughtfulness, as, in her experience, the reverse usually applied.

Jo knew Paul was not very romantic, nor particularly tactful, but he was a nice person. They had nothing apart from work in common, yet they got on well.

Understandably, they talked a lot about the job but around this they also managed to talk about their lives, loves and dreams.

Jo was a dog lover and had a very cute cocker spaniel called Sadie. With her work commitments this was difficult but she was lucky to have her mother to help out. Jo had once been engaged but cancelled the wedding with two weeks to go, when she found out that her fiancé had been seeing her best friend—as the old joke goes, where would she find another best friend?

This experience made her overly cautious about men, but she truly thought that Paul would be an exception. Paul was shy and quiet but serious and sincere. He told Jo of his marriage and its break-up. She wondered whether the bad marriage had scared him off relationships completely. Paul had been married for two years to Jane who had turned out not to be the quiet, shy girl he'd thought she was. In fact, she spoke a lot on the subject of what she most wanted, and that was to change him. Paul was resistant to change… and there was the rub.

Jo, on the other hand, liked the fact that Paul was a bit odd. What she most liked was his passion for his work and his straightforward manner; you always knew where you stood with him. Jo talked of her promotion ambition; she had already passed her sergeants' exam, she had done acting DS duties and wanted to get on. Paul was supportive and encouraging and didn't feel at all threatened by Jo's plans.

Their evening went well, and Jo felt that they'd made a connection. At the end of the date, Paul drove Jo home.

As her car was at the station, Paul offered to pick Jo up in the morning and she happily accepted. Paul was a perfect gentleman and they kissed on the cheek when he dropped her off.

Jo was glad and touched that he was taking it slowly, but she was determined to make things progress. She liked Paul even more for being respectful towards her, but she didn't want to lose momentum and thought that he'd probably need a bit of a push.

Chapter 17

Alan was delighted but surprised to find that the local authority had already appointed a replacement for Luke. Maybe because of Aaron's death they felt obliged to better support the home, so they moved faster than usual. In any case, it was good to have enough staff to run the home properly, without putting too much stress on everyone else.

"Hi, I'm Laurence." Alan turned around in his chair to see a young man in his early twenties standing just inside the door.

This must be the new support worker to replace Luke, thought Alan. He was about five feet eight, very slim with a shock of unruly fair hair.

Laurence Cook was a cover name; he'd been given a back story, or "legend" which Laurence now trotted out for Alan. Laurence said that he'd done his social work degree in Falmouth (half-true) but came from Swinton so wanted to work nearer to his parents, as they were frail and elderly (in truth they would be offended, being fit and healthy). This was Laurence's first job and he was excited;

he was keen to work with the young people and make a difference.

Alan only half listened to Laurence, having had so many care workers come and go, all arriving with the same high level of enthusiasm.

Alan smiled weakly, "Welcome to Manningsbrook. I'll introduce you to everyone and give you a tour at the same time."

Alan started in the lounge area where Finn was playing Nintendo and a couple of others were playing cards. "It's an inset day," Alan explained when he saw Laurence's quizzical look.

"This is Laurence," Alan said to the three children, "he's Luke's replacement, and has started today."

Laurence was greeted by blank, disinterested stares. Alan continued talking, "This is Finn, he's the oldest here, if you want to know anything, ask Finn."

Laurence smiled warmly at Finn who stared blankly for a moment, then resumed his game. The tour continued and Laurence got a feel for the place. Laurence felt an undercurrent there, but maybe this was understandable, bearing in mind recent events. All the staff, including Alan, were friendly enough but seemed to be still in shock from the death of Aaron.

The house and grounds were large and impressive but although newly painted, were shabby and not well maintained. It was fairly bog-standard as care homes go but was nicely situated on the edge of Leeston.

When the tour was finished Laurence sought out Sophie to talk to. Sophie was in the kitchen making tea, "Do you want a drink, Laurence?"

"I'd love a tea, milk no sugar, please," said Laurence. "So why did the last guy, Luke leave?"

"Honestly, I don't know. He seemed perfectly happy here, he took his job very seriously. I don't know why he would want to go?"

"Was he sacked?"

"I don't know, one minute, things were fine, then he was gone. Alan isn't saying anything, but I don't know. I tried to message Luke, but he hasn't replied. I can't think of any reason why he'd be sacked unless it's something to do with Aaron."

"Aaron?"

"The boy who died recently. Why are you asking?" Sophie said.

"No reason," said Laurence, "I suppose I just want to find my feet. We'll be on the same rota?"

"Yes, I guess."

"Good." Laurence gave Sophie his most winning smile and she relaxed slightly.

Laurence continued on his way round the home and found Finn, still playing Nintendo. Laurence knew nothing about gaming but saw two tough-looking animated characters fighting on the TV screen.

"Finn isn't it?" said Laurence cheerfully.

Finn didn't respond he just carried on playing. The two characters were kicking and punching the living daylights out of each other in an enclosed ring. Laurence was thinking that this was not an entirely healthy game to play, but instead said, "I don't know this game, what are you playing?"

Finn responded monosyllabically, "UFC."

"What's that?"

"The Ultimate Fighting Championship, it's mixed martial arts; it's really sick." Finn warmed up with enthusiasm.

"Sounds sick," said Laurence, knowing full well that 'sick' in this context meant good, although he privately thought it would equally apply to the traditional meaning. "Who are you?"

"Conor McGregor, he's my hero. He don't take no shit… sorry about that."

"No problem, no one should have to take any shit." Laurence looked serious.

Finn looked at Laurence properly for the first time, "You're right, they shouldn't." He then looked away quickly.

"OK, well I'll see you around," said Laurence brightly.

"All right," agreed Finn, focusing on the screen.

That evening DC Harry Thomson, also known as social worker Laurence, reported in to DI Sue Taylor by phone. He told her about his first day, going into as much detail as possible.

"The manager, Alan, has been there a long time and seems to have a grip on the place. I met Finn and I think I've made some progress with him. He's a troubled boy, and it may take a while to get through to him."

“What about the others?”

“The staff I met seem nice, I don’t get the same feeling as Finn from the other kids. I don’t think the other kids know anything, but I’ll keep on digging. I’ve got some night cover coming up, so I’ll get some opportunities to talk to them on their own.”

Sue struggled to remain patient, she knew that this could take a while, and that there was no rushing it. “OK, just make sure we keep in touch. Same time tomorrow?”

“Of course.”

Chapter 18

The internet is quite amazing. With a little digging you can find almost anything you need, including How to Make A Bomb; yes, that's the search I used, simple as that. For five years I've been going crazy, thinking about what those filthy paedo bastards did to me. They damaged my body but worse, they messed with my mind. I know that I had been hurt, but I still have huge gaps in my memory. I can remember some things, but so much I still can't. Was that the drugs or the alcohol?

The Zodiac Club; they think they're so smart with their stupid code names and secrecy, but I now know who they all are. They thought they could stay hidden, but I found out. It took some time, but it was worth the effort. Before, I knew their faces and their code names but now I know who every one of those very "respectable" gentlemen are, where they live and where they work. They are made up of the supposed great and the good; a policeman, a vicar, a care home manager, a politician and two businessmen. Two of them have even got wives and children; how do they square that? How do they go about their normal lives, knowing what they get up to?

So, I ordered all the materials online, but from separate suppliers, so as not to arouse suspicion. The stuff arrived at my bedsit in dribs and drabs with no one the wiser. I was using mobile phones as detonators to keep control of the explosions, so I got some cheap ones from the market.

As a care leaver I was lucky to get my own flat, and had a job arranged for me doing waiting for a café, in Swinton. Having escaped the home at 16, I was out of their clutches; in reality, they were losing interest in me as I got older. I endured years of abuse but now it would be my chance to get my own back.

Around work I had time to stake out the flat and follow my tormentors, as best as I could on a stolen bike. From my cycling, the internet and patient watching, I was able to build a good picture of the men… I could be a spy. Luckily, they were all fairly local. From this work I managed to identify every one of them and then thought about what to do about it.

Putting a bomb together was easy, there was even a YouTube video to help. The hardest thing was working out how much explosive I needed; that, and not blowing myself up.

My plan was simple, to give them some of what they gave me — absolute fear.

Watching my first target was easy; I selected Scorpio first because I thought he'd be an easy target. Scorpio, real name Peter Calder, was a businessman who lived in a small hamlet just outside of Leeston. He had a large, detached cottage with a long driveway and the parking was away from the house. He drove a brand-new, silver, five series BMW. He was married with two young children, which makes it worse, that he is such a hypocrite.

It was easy to watch the house from a spot off a nearby public footpath without being seen. For a long time, I tracked the comings and goings of the house, building up a pattern of movement. I had planned this like a military operation, not least because I'd had so long to think about it.

On the big day I sneaked in at about four a.m. with my bomb and hid it under the car. I then went to my hiding place and waited patiently. It was a fresh, bright night with a full moon staring down at me. I was so afraid but also exhilarated by what I was doing. I was hyper-vigilant, hearing, seeing, smelling everything around… I thought this must be what a fox feels. Yes, I am the fox. I could hear small animals rustling around the fields and woods, and what sounded like a scream. But I wasn't fazed, because tonight *I* was the predator. The night smelled different, more real; the musty-sweet odour of the woods filled my nostrils.

On time, at seven thirty, Scorpio came out of the house. As expected, he was dressed for work in jacket and trousers. In my hiding place I knew I was invisible, but I instinctively ducked down lower. I clutched my mobile phone ready to call the number of the phone to activate my bomb. When he was about twenty metres from the car, I pressed call. There was a moment's pause when it felt like everything had stopped, then suddenly a huge explosion hit the car. I saw Scorpio fall to the ground and I hoped that he wasn't dead; after all, I wanted him to be afraid. I wanted the fear to eat into his soul; I wanted him to always be looking over his shoulder, not to get off that lightly. Although I was a long way away, my ears were ringing from the noise of the explosion. The car was still standing but was on fire. Smaller bits of the car had been scattered in a shower of debris.

I saw Scorpio move, so that was a relief. The revenge plan had officially started and seemed to have begun successfully. His wife ran out of the house in her dressing gown and rushed to his aid. If only she knew what he was really like, would she care so much? As the dust settled, they hobbled back to the house where the children stood transfixed at the doorway.

I cycled away with the vision of them hugging each other fixed in my mind. As I cycled, keeping to the bridle paths and back ways home, I heard the sound of sirens. I knew where they were going. I smiled to myself, satisfied with my night's work.

Arriving home, I was sweating profusely; could they possibly trace the explosion back to me? No way, I'd been too careful. Anyway, I was abused such a long time ago, they'd probably forgotten all about me. I'd been patient, kept my head down, done my research; now it was time for them to pay.

My next target would be Aries, the Very Reverend Clive Owen, the vicar of Leeston parish church on the outskirts of town. The church was ancient; it was built in the Norman style with cut stone and huge vaulted ceilings. Through a porch, a large doorway made up of concentric arches led to the narthex, then on to the nave. The interior was not extravagant but had a quiet, peaceful feeling to it.

To the left of the church was a four-bedroomed Victorian house, which served as the vicarage for the vicar. Aries lived there alone but had a daily housekeeper who saw to his needs, or at least the domestic ones. His car was parked at the front on a small gravel drive. It was harder to keep surveillance on the rectory as the area was busy, near the High Street. Looking inconspicuous at the rear of the cemetery, pretending to look at the gravestones, I could see enough of the pattern of his life to form a plan.

Chapter 19

"An explosion, really?" Detective Inspector Sue Taylor was taking a call from the control room in her office. "Have the forensic crime scene manager meet me there, please call DS Smith, get him to send a couple of DCs along as well."

Sue put the phone down and started to think about this next challenge. *Could this be accidental? And if not, why? Was it an accident, terrorism or a grudge?*

She walked through the station, it was only eight a.m. and the building was starting to get going. She said good morning to anyone she saw, going over in her head what she'd been told. A car had been blown up on the drive of a private house in a rural area, not far from Leeston. No one was seriously hurt, thankfully, but there was no motive known yet.

When Sue arrived in her Mercedes at the scene of the explosion, she saw that the Crime Scene Manager, Dave Johnson, was chatting to a man and a woman who were standing next to a smouldering BMW. It was a clear, bright, cold morning, and the house was set in beautiful grounds backing onto the heart of Leeston Forest. The fire service and ambulance service had already left before Sue arrived. The fire service had extinguished the fire and the ambulance crew had left Peter wrapped in a blanket.

As Sue walked up to the group, Dave Johnson introduced Sue to Peter and Naomi Calder, who were clearly both in shock.

Naomi was crying while Peter was ashen with several small cuts on his face. He was mute whilst his wife talked at speed.

"Why has this happened, someone tried to kill my husband? Why would this happen to us, we're normal people?"

Dave called Sue to one side, "I haven't told them, but it looks like it was an improvised explosive device under the car, probably set off remotely by someone nearby. I'll know more when we get back to the lab and look at what we've got. I've told HQ and they've called Special Branch in case it's terrorism."

Sue nodded, "OK, thanks for letting me know."

Sue left Dave to his search and walked back to Peter and Naomi. Sue asked, "Is there any reason anyone may have a grudge against you?"

Peter stared blankly, but Naomi answered for him, "Of course not, we don't have any reason to upset people. My husband's factory makes plastic containers, they don't hurt anyone."

Sue looked at Peter who just slowly shook his head. Sue led them indoors as the forensics team arrived, leaving Dave to do his work. The exterior of the house was impressive and charming, and the interior did not disappoint. The house was tastefully decorated in a modern style with good quality furniture. *These people certainly lived well*, thought Sue. Sue spotted two young children poking their heads around the corner of the dark wood stairway banister. They were aged about ten or twelve, a boy and a girl. As Sue spotted them, they ducked back, and she heard a scramble as they ran back upstairs.

"Stay upstairs you two!" shouted Naomi from the kitchen as she put the kettle on. She then came out and looked at Sue. "Coffee or tea?"

"Coffee please. Milk, no sugar."

When they had drinks, they all sat on the sumptuous leather sofa in the lounge. Sue took details of their lives, friends, colleagues and associates, trying to find any motive for what had happened. Sue was a bit surprised to find a couple of names she knew on his list of friends, but that was probably understandable because they were so active in the community. They were church-goers, Rotarians, Women's Institute and golf club members; they were obviously sociable and involved in community affairs.

There was nothing in either of their backgrounds to suggest any reason why they should be targeted. Could it be a case of mistaken identity? But that would be a huge mistake to make and seemed unlikely. So, there must have been a motive, what secrets were being hidden by this apparently perfect family? Maybe their phone and internet activity would provide clues.

When Sue left the house two of her detectives arrived to take statements. Sue said goodbye to the couple with a faintly uneasy feeling she couldn't quite put her finger on.

Chapter 20

Laurence walked into the lounge where he saw Finn sat on the sofa talking to the new boy, Simon. He was a lot younger than Finn, only nine years old, so it was kind of Finn to take him under his wing. They stopped talking abruptly as Laurence approached them. They had been whispering together, so Laurence said cheerfully, "What are you two up to?"

Simon looked startled but Finn replied coolly, "Just getting to know Simon, and making him feel welcome."

"Do you guys fancy taking my boat out? I've got a small boat moored in the marina. I can teach you to sail if you like," Laurence said cheerfully.

"We don't like water," said Finn bluntly.

"Simon?" said Laurence.

Simon looked sheepish and mumbled, "No thanks."

"So, what do you guys want to do, we've got the afternoon free and everyone else is busy," Laurence persisted.

"Well the new Star Wars movie is on, but I know you won't take us there," Finn said in a surly tone.

"That's where you're wrong, let me see what time it's on and I'll book some tickets."

The boys' eyes lit up, "Do you mean it?" they chorused.

"Yeah," said Laurence, "let's do it."

"You know you're all right… for a social worker," said Finn.

"You're all right yourself," Laurence smiled.

The afternoon was a complete success, the boys loved the film and they came out of the cinema energised and excited. They even stopped for a burger afterwards, which was entirely unheard of. Finn tried to offer to pay but Laurence refused, wondering how Finn could even have the money to do so.

Laurence also had a great time and thought, with some regret, of his failed social work career. Mind you, if he could save these boys from coming to harm, it would be a job well done.

The three drove back to the home chatting excitedly about the movie. The boys could relate to Luke Skywalker, each having lost their parents one way or another. They imagined themselves heirs to special powers and having the ability to do great things. Finn was beginning to become worried, though, that he was already on the dark side of The Force.

When they arrived at the home, they were greeted by a furious Alan Rogers. "Where the hell have you been?" he glared at Laurence aggressively.

Laurence was cool, "We went to the cinema, the boys were at a loose end and everyone else was busy."

"You can't just do that..."

"Why?"

"There's no budget for that type of trip," Alan blustered.

"I know, that's why I paid myself," declared Laurence.

"What... but..." Alan retorted, feeling wrong-footed.

"I've got a bit of spare money from my birthday and wanted a treat. I wanted to see the movie, I just needed someone to go with me."

Finn overheard the exchange and was impressed by Laurence's generosity, and for standing up to Alan. Alan was less impressed; he turned around and stormed back to the house, saying nothing else.

Laurence turned to Finn and Simon, who just stood staring at him. "Well thanks for the afternoon boys, see you later."

Finn and Simon went into the lounge and sat down together. Finn thought for a moment then said, "Do you want a new phone?"

Simon looked confused, "Yes, but how come?"

"You just need to come somewhere with me next week where you can get a phone for nothing."

Of course, Finn said "nothing", but was it really?

Simon was excited, "Do you mean it, can I really have a phone?"

"Yeah, of course, anything for my little bro'."

Chapter 21

The Zodiac Club members met in the flat on the next Wednesday afternoon. Although it was still quite cool, the late afternoon sun shone pale, on a cloudless day, belying the gloomy mood of the group. There were no boys there in the flat as this was a business meeting, not pleasure.

Scorpio was red in the face and looked dishevelled, as he said, "Someone tried to kill me, it must be something to do with the club."

Capricorn responded, "There is no evidence of that. The police have no idea…"

"No change there then," Aries chimed in.

Capricorn continued, "But it was definitely a home-made device, probably detonated by a mobile phone."

Taurus chipped in, "There is no talk in the home about the bomb, so I suggest that there's no connection there."

"Probably something to do with your business," suggested Aries.

"Most importantly, the police are not making any link between Aaron's death, the bombing or any of us," declared Capricorn.

Pisces changed the subject, "So when do we start club meetings again?"

Capricorn said, "Well there's no reason not to start again. How about next week? Has Finn found a replacement boy?"

"We've got a new boy, Simon, he's just arrived. Finn has already prepared him to come along to the club. He seems… malleable," replied Taurus.

Libra stepped in, "OK, do we all agree? We re-start the club next week, the usual time. Let's get on with life."

They all happily agreed and got ready to leave, with little small talk. By the time they left it was evening and the sun had gone down. They left separately, going their own ways, little knowing that they were being watched and that their world was about to be rocked further.

As I watch them each leave in turn, I wait, hidden, for my next target. You know, I genuinely enjoy this part, the surveillance you might call it. There he is, that fat little bastard Aries, so pompous and self-righteous, a man of God, a vicar. Well, I have a surprise in my rucksack for him.

I followed him at a distance as he hurriedly walked back towards the church. He hurried through the "Trees" estate as though he was expecting to be mugged. When he cleared the estate he noticeably slowed down as if he now felt safe. Walking slowly along the High Street he paused to look in several shop windows, then looked around as if sensing he was being followed. But he couldn't possibly see me, I was being way too careful.

Aries turned left off of the High Street into Church Lane; I held back to let him get a fair way down the quarter mile long road leading to the church of the Holy Trinity. As you turn left from the High Street into Church Lane there are a few shops including a jeweller, an estate agent and café, now closed. The shops soon peter out to become light woodland. The road starts as cobblestones but becomes an unmade road halfway down the lane. As I reached the corner, I saw Aries scurrying along, obviously in a hurry again. I jogged slowly, keeping to the shadows, making sure I could keep him in sight.

I saw him arrive at the vicarage, where his 2014 plated Mini was parked outside. I saw him go up the few steps to the front door, quickly look around, then slip inside. Excellent.

I found a nice, well-hidden spot in the graveyard with a good view of the car and the front door. It was nine p.m. but I didn't want to miss Aries, so I sat down and settled in for a long night. I opened my rucksack to reveal the device, a torch, a flask and some sandwiches.

The night seemed to last forever; there was one bit of excitement when a small group of drunk teenagers came out of the pub. They wobbled their way towards the church laughing and joking with each other. I heard one of the boys dare someone to go into the cemetery. But suddenly a light blazed brightly on the side of the vicarage, the teenagers fled back up Church Lane back to the safety of town.

This was good luck for me; I hadn't been discovered and I had found out that there was a passive infrared light on the side that I'd need to avoid. I set my phone to wake me up at four, on vibrate, in case I overslept. I sat and thought and remembered.

I was twelve when I arrived at Manningsbrook Children's Home. No, arrived sounds wrong… when I was sent, unwanted to the home. I went there because my parents died. They died in a freak car crash, on the way back from shopping, when a lorry came across the central reservation and wiped them out. The driver had fallen asleep at the wheel, having driven across Europe the day before. I should have been with them, but I moaned until my parents let me see a friend instead of going with them. I still feel guilty about that, as if I could have done anything.

I was an only child and social services tried to house me with my aunt, but she was having none of it. She already had two children of her own and a husband who'd left, so I have some sympathy, but I was devastated, and I felt unwanted.

I was angry when I first went to the home but the kindness, care and attention of the care home manager, Alan Rogers, turned my life around again. To be honest that is almost the worst thing… I trusted him and he betrayed that trust. He was friendly to me just so that he and his paedo friends could have some fun. Well, he's going to pay, they're all going to pay.

That's why I'm here, sat in a graveyard, in the middle of the night. I must have fallen asleep because the next thing I know I was awoken by the vibration of my phone. It was four a.m., pitch black and eerily quiet. I'm not afraid, though, I am the hunter, not the hunted. I crept out of my hiding place like the fox I'd become. I was aware of the security light, so I skirted around to avoid setting it off. I got to the Mini and jumped as I heard a sudden crashing sound from the direction of the High Street. The bomb was still in my rucksack and I took it out carefully, arming the device. I then placed it, nervously, behind the rear nearside wheel, making sure that it was out of sight.

I retraced my steps back to my hiding place and settled down to wait again. If Aries followed his normal pattern, he would walk to the shop to get a newspaper at eight a.m. I set my alarm for seven and tried to rest, but couldn't, I was too pumped up. Apart from seeing the odd wild animal (I even saw a badger scuttle across the lane) there was nothing of interest and the night dragged on.

I awoke at seven with the alarm and took a moment trying to work out where I was. Waking up in the middle of a dream where I was being buried alive, I was terrified to find that I was in a graveyard. By the time I got my bearings again and my head cleared, my heart had stopped pounding.

I checked my phone, making sure it was ready to go to detonate the bomb. I had some of my sandwiches and some coffee… a bizarre picnic… and felt a lot better. I started to feel the now familiar combination of excitement and fear.

At eight a.m. I was wound up as tight as a violin, but he didn't appear. At first, I was quite cool about it, thinking he'll be out in a second. But by eight thirty I was getting seriously worried; he was normally a creature of habit, what had changed today? I must have become distracted because suddenly I realised that Aries was out of the door and walking towards the driveway. In a panic I pressed the button to send the call to detonate, but I was too late, the delay meant that Aries was next to the Mini when it exploded. The force of the explosion knocked Aries off his feet and he was thrown away from the car, like a doll being thrown in a child's tantrum.

The car was on fire and smoke started to billow, but there was now an unnerving silence. I came to my senses and ran over to check on Aries. He was lying on his back, arms and legs at unnatural angles, blood coming from several cuts and an ugly gash in his head. He seemed not to be breathing but his eyes were wide open, staring heavenward. I suspected that would not be his destination.

Now I realised that it was time to get out of there; I could already see some activity from the other end of the lane, and I heard a distant siren. I almost left, then somehow, using some instinct of self-preservation I remembered that my rucksack was still in the graveyard. I ran over and grabbed it, then made for the woods at the rear of the High Street, taking cover as the first curious bystanders started to make their way to the church.

I worked my way through the woods keeping cover until I could slip out onto the High Street. Conscious of the town's CCTV system, I put my hoody up over my baseball cap, completely covering my face. I walked slowly, so as not to draw attention to myself, and headed to where I had chained up my bike.

As I cycled out of Leeston towards home I felt an all-encompassing feeling of elation. I hadn't intended to kill Aries, but that didn't mean that I regretted it. The fact is, he is now dead, and I cannot bring myself to grieve for that.

Chapter 22

Sue hurriedly drove to the scene of the explosion. The weather was grey but dry and there was a slight chill in the air, the sort of weather that forebodes bad weather on the way. The area had been cordoned off at the junction with the High Street and a crowd had gathered, in spite of the threat of bad weather. There were news crews there already and she wondered, not for the first time, how they found out about this so quickly.

Logging in with the scene guard, the forensics team were waiting for her by the wreckage. The explosion had also damaged the vicarage, breaking the windows nearest the front door. Walking past the burnt-out shell of a car, Sue saw the lifeless body of the former vicar of Leeston parish church. He was lying on his back with his arms and legs spread at impossible angles.

Sue saw that the Crime Scene Manager, Dave Johnson, was talking to one of the forensics team and headed towards him. Dave indicated that they should take cover in the capacious porch of the vicarage. They immediately got down to their business

"What do you think?" asked Sue.

Dave marshalled his thoughts, then said, "I think it's the same bomb-maker as the last one; it's a similar site for the explosion, under the car, and just quickly looking around it looks like the same components. Of course, we'll need to confirm this when we get to the lab, but it's a good working hypothesis."

"Thanks, that's all we need, a crazy bomber on the loose." Dave looked pained, and Sue added, "I know it's not your fault, it's just a bit busy at the moment."

As they spoke, a uniformed officer walked up the lane with a middle-aged woman who suddenly started to wail on seeing the deceased cleric.

The officer steered the distraught woman over to Sue, "Sorry ma'am, this is the housekeeper, she was on her way to work. I thought you'd want to see her immediately?"

"Of course," said Sue, "get her inside and get the kettle on to make her a cup of tea, I'll be in soon."

Sue looked around; if it were the same bomb as used last time, it was remotely detonated, so where could you hide to get a good view without being seen?

She looked at the graveyard and immediately saw that it was perfect, she was sure that's where the bomber had hidden. Sue instructed that there must be a fingertip search of the graveyard, anything that may have been dropped was to be seized. It is surprising (but fortuitous) that, sometimes, people will leave cigarette butts, sweet wrappers or drinks cans at the scene of a crime. Fingerprints or DNA found on these items may not be conclusive evidence but may give clues to identify suspects or corroborate other evidence.

Sue walked into the vicarage and found the housekeeper in the kitchen with an officer. The housekeeper surprised her by saying, "I'm not going to pretend, he really wasn't a nice man, but it's still a shock, how could this happen?"

Sue replied, "We still need to work out what happened, but is there any reason why anyone would want to harm Reverend Owen?"

The housekeeper looked shocked, "You mean this wasn't some terrible accident?"

"No, it was a bombing, and someone must have a motive to have done it."

"Why would anyone do such a thing? He was pompous and rude to people, but that's no reason to kill someone, he didn't have any enemies unless you include the bishop."

"The bishop?"

"Yes, I heard them arguing once because Clive wouldn't cover another parish, the bishop called him a "little shit!", not very religious, I thought."

"Perhaps not grounds for murder, though?"

"Perhaps not," conceded the housekeeper.

Sue drove back to the office, her mind buzzing with thoughts. What was the connection between the reverend and Peter Calder? Why was one killed but not the other? Who would do such a thing and why?

Chapter 23

DC Jo James stood patiently in DI Sue Taylor's office as she finished her conversation with her DS, Paul Smith, who had started to set up a major enquiry room for the bombings. A child murder and two bombings at once? Thank God it was so quiet here in the country, she smiled to herself, thinking of the piss taking she took from colleagues for working in "sleepy old" Leeston Forest. Sue gestured for Jo to sit down.

When she finished her call, Sue smiled and said, "How can I help you, Jo?"

Jo smiled back, "I thought you'd like to know, there's been a breakthrough, we have two witnesses who saw a small white van pull out of the car park, on the night of the murder, near the deposition site. They'd gone to the car park to talk because they'd had an argument. As they drove in, the van pulled away in a hurry and left."

"Could it be a courting couple?"

Jo shook her head, "That's the thing, he says that there were at least three men in the van."

"Same question, but a courting trio?"

"True, it's possible, but the witness says it didn't look right, he thinks they were surprised to be seen and looked guilty."

"Can they describe the men?" asked Sue.

"Not well… all white males and middle-aged. The witnesses say that they seemed to want to get out too quickly when they arrived."

"Were they locals; did the witnesses recognise them?" Sue pressed.

"They may be locals in the van, but the witnesses weren't, they're from Swinton so wouldn't know."

"What about the van?"

"They say it was old, small and white."

"OK, that narrows it down, we need to know how many old, small, white vans there are in the area. We need statements from the witnesses and get them to do an E-fit; it would be useful to get pictures of the suspects we can publicise. Once we've got those done, I'll do a press release, that will shake something out." Sue's enthusiasm grew as she warmed to the topic, this could be a breakthrough, at least it was something to go on. So far there was nothing from the covert operation, so it was nice to get a lead.

Jo came back an hour later, "I've booked the witnesses into E-fit, and got a print out of all small white vans over ten years old within a twenty-mile radius. We're looking at around a hundred using that criteria; I'll get some research going to see if anything leaps out, although from a quick scan, five of them are registered to known sex offenders."

"That's great, thanks, obviously this is a priority." Sue was impressed by Jo's initiative and was happy that she was on her team. Jo started to leave when Sue called out, "Jo, remind me to let us have a talk about your future when all this is over. I really value your work here, but I assume you want to get on?"

"That would be really good, thanks, I'd appreciate it," said Jo, beaming a huge smile.

Jo's happiness gave Sue a warm feeling; she was thinking that things were going fine, even though she was juggling investigating a murder and two bombings, she still had time to think about her staff. Unfortunately, at that moment the phone rang, the call shattered her reverie, it was Detective Chief Superintendent Alan Scotty Irvine.

"Hello Sue, I gather it's getting hot down there, how are you coping?"

This was typical of Scotty, a large Glaswegian in his fifties, he was a dyed-in-the-wool misogynist and resented having a woman as one of his senior detectives. He always took any opportunity to undermine her; today was no different. He continued, "I'll be sending DCI Jones down to take over," he said, "I assume you have no problem with that? You two seemed to work well before."

Sue wondered if he knew about her and Steve's relationship, but decided he didn't because he would never have allowed them to work together if he did. In fact, she'd be grateful for the help, and she liked working with Steve. "No, no problem at all," she said.

“Well, that’s all right then,” he replied hanging up, but Sue could sense his disappointment at not being able to rattle her.

Sue immediately picked up her mobile and phoned Steve, “It’s your lucky day,” she said.

“I’ve won the lottery?” laughed Steve.

“Close, we’re working together again. Scotty just called saying he was assigning you to come down and take over.”

Steve snorted with indignation, “Well I won’t take over, but it will be nice to work together again… that is, if you’re OK with it?”

Sue thought for a moment and realised that she didn’t mind at all. “No, actually I could really do with some help here.”

“That’s great then, I’ll bring some more DCs as well,” said Steve brightly, “I’ll see you soon.” With that they hung up, both feeling that their relationship had taken a step forward.

Chapter 24

DC Harry Thomson, also known as Laurence the social worker, was really settling in well at the home. He loved the febrile atmosphere of barely controlled mayhem. He hadn't realised how much he missed the hustle and bustle of this kind of environment... and he was growing fond of the kids. Alan Rogers was an excellent manager who, if a little remote with staff, obviously cared deeply about his charges. Laurence had become close to Finn and, although he hadn't got to the bottom of what it might be, he was sure that Finn wanted to tell him something. Finn was disturbed and afraid, but Laurence felt that he was getting close to talking.

As Laurence was walking towards the kitchen the front door opened and a tall, smart, uniformed policeman entered the house. He saw Laurence and there seemed to be a moment of surprise in his eyes, but this quickly passed.

The policeman stepped forward, holding out his hand, "Hello, I'm Inspector Jon Thorne, I don't think we've met."

"Hi, I'm Laurence, no I'm new here, can I help you?" Laurence was surprised that the inspector had let himself in with a key but said nothing.

"No, I'm here to see Alan; I'm the liaison officer for the home. After the recent tragedy, I wanted to see how everyone was getting on."

"OK, I guess you know the way then, I'll see you around."

Laurence walked on, thinking nothing more of the encounter. For his part, Jon Thorne felt troubled. He knew that there was a new staff member appointed after Luke left but for some reason Laurence looked familiar. On seeing Alan, he forgot this concern and they chatted amiably about the issues concerning the home. Jon Thorne knew that it was important to have good relations with children's homes for a number of reasons: that children in care often go missing or they may become involved in crime, or they may be vulnerable to sexual exploitation. Thorne had been the inspector in Leeston for a long time and knew pretty much everything significant that was going on.

He prided himself on his connections and was well known and well respected, both within the police and outside. He was an active church member and was involved in a couple of local charities through the Freemasons; in fact, he was an absolute paragon of the community.

That evening Laurence, the social worker, went home, then as DC Harry Johnson, he reported to DI Taylor the events of the day. Sue Taylor was frustrated that so little progress was being made but was encouraged that Harry was establishing a rapport with Finn. Now she wanted him to push harder, to exploit that friendship and get some concrete information from the boy. Sue was impatient for results and gave him one more week or she'd pull him out. Sue sensed that Harry was uneasy, and asked, "Are you OK?"

"Yeah, sure," Harry replied unconvincingly. "Just so that you know, I saw a police officer, an Inspector Thorne at the home; he said he was there for liaison. I'm sure I haven't met him before, and I don't think I've been compromised."

"Are you sure you're OK to carry on doing this?" Sue was conscious that undercover officers can sometimes suffer psychological problems or maybe go native, perhaps due to the loss of identity caused by the total immersion of their lives into a false world. She was aware of his past history and was worried that this assignment was affecting him.

Harry was firm, "Yes, of course I'm OK; I know what I need to do."

After he'd finished the debrief, though, Harry felt troubled. Being in the home was dragging up lots of once-forgotten feelings. He didn't like lying to Finn and was wondering whether he had made the right career move by joining the police. He was surprised to find that he really missed social care. The thought of exploiting Finn's vulnerability made him feel uneasy; he wasn't keen on tricking him into helping by betraying his trust. Harry understood the mission, but he also saw himself in Finn and knew how he would have felt in the same position.

"First Scorpio's BMW was blown up and now Aries has been murdered."

A shaken Capricorn had phoned Taurus that evening in a panic. "On top of this, I have to tell you I recognise your new staff member, Laurence. He's not a social worker; he is an undercover policeman."

"I know, I feel like things are getting out of hand, someone is terrorising us. Now we find out there is a spy in the camp. Why didn't you say anything earlier about Laurence?" asked Taurus.

"I've only just realised what was going on. He must be undercover because they suspect a connection with the home! That brings it closer to us, we need to act now; he's been grooming the kids for information, particularly Finn."

"I thought the local authority were a bit quick sending a replacement," Taurus pondered, "what are we going to do?"

"Don't worry, I know what to do but I'll need some help. Have you got his address? We'll need a few of us."

"I'll phone Pisces to meet us at ten."

Chapter 25

The following morning Sue and Steve sat in Sue's office, drinking coffee. They had agreed that Sue would continue running the Aaron murder while Steve would lead the bombing investigations. Steve, because of his senior rank, had overall responsibility but he knew how good a detective she was and saw their roles as equal.

They had split the teams into two distinct enquiries and, with extra staff, Leeston station was overflowing with people. Sue was happy with this arrangement, not least because she had another opportunity to work with Steve. She was feeling upbeat and positive, but that was about to change.

Inspector Jon Thorne knocked on her door and stepped inside, "I wouldn't ordinarily trouble you, Sue, but there's been a suicide by a member of staff from Manningsbrook Children's Home."

Sue's blood ran cold, but she managed to ask, "Who?"

"One of the social workers," Thorne continued, "It's not connected to your investigation because he wasn't even there when Aaron was killed, so he couldn't have been involved."

Her face was ashen, "What is his name?"

"He only recently arrived, he replaced Luke, who had to be sacked."

"What is his name?" said Sue, louder than she had intended.

"Laurence something, I think. The day turn Sergeant Roz attended, there were no suspicious circumstances, so you weren't called. Did you want to speak to Roz, she's in the canteen, I'll get her?"

As Jon Thorne walked towards the canteen, Sue's mind raced. Can this be true, has Harry killed himself, did she push him too hard? He did sound odd yesterday. A wave of guilt washed over her, and she felt nauseous.

Steve was looking at her curiously, "Are you OK, Sue? You look like you've seen a ghost."

"I… I… I'm not sure… I think something terrible has happened."

Roz walked into the office with Jon Thorne, "Can I help ma'am?"

Sue could barely speak, "You've been to a sudden death today?"

Roz replied, "Yes, a young social worker from the care home has hanged himself. Pressure of work, I suppose."

"How did this come about?"

"Well, the home called when he didn't turn up for work today, so we broke into his flat and found him hanging from a rope tied to the top of the wardrobe. The funny thing is that we couldn't find any personal items in the flat; it was more like a hotel room."

"What have you done with the scene?"

"Nothing, the body's gone, it was suicide, he left a typed note saying just one word: "SORRY". Inspector Thorne came to the scene and agreed with my assessment; have I done something wrong?"

"No, of course not." Sue's brain went into overload, how could this be? Her eyes started to well up with tears, she blamed herself; she knew Harry was not happy, why did she not just pull him out?

Roz looked worried, "Is everything all right?"

Sue felt bereft but spoke through her tears, "No, not really, you mustn't tell anyone yet, but he was an undercover police officer working for me. I think I pushed him too far."

Roz was shocked. "Sorry, I didn't know."

Sue's mind was racing, "You wouldn't have known. Can you put the paperwork through me, I don't know how to handle this? I've got to tell someone."

Steve saw that Sue was upset.

Steve looked at Roz who just looked down and muttered, "Sorry, I should go now." With this, Roz left the office.

Steve sat down saying nothing, knowing that Sue would speak when she was ready. After a few minutes Sue said, "I think I got something badly wrong." She went on to tell Steve what had happened, "What should I do?"

Steve considered for a while then said carefully. "Sue, I have a different view of this than you. Look you're investigating murder, you put someone in undercover and they die. What would *I* conclude? Not that he committed suicide, he's much more likely to have been murdered."

At that point, the phone rang. Sue instinctively knew that it would be Scotty Irvine.

"What the hell are you doing down there?" shouted DCS Irvine belligerently before she could even say hello, "One of my people has committed suicide on your watch; I am bloody furious."

Once again Sue wondered what his sources were, she remained cool. "I'm just briefing the DCI, he's here now."

"Good, put him on!"

There was a slight pause as Steve took the phone. "Keep her away from the investigation; I've called the Independent Police Complaints Commission; this looks very bad for us. I'm just glad that you're now in charge. Frankly, I'm not surprised something like this has happened, she's too clever for her own good."

"Very well, sir, but I think it's more likely murder rather than suicide," said Steve flatly and hung up before Scotty could say anything else. *He'll be fuming,* thought Steve, but he also knew that Scotty often relied on him and wouldn't openly challenge what he was saying.

"What did he say?" asked Sue.

"Just that he wanted to be kept updated," Steve lied. He had no intention of taking Sue off the case, not because she was his girlfriend but because she was an excellent detective and essential to the investigation. "Now let's see what we've got."

Sue explained what she felt was the pressure she had put on Harry to get a result, even though she sensed his reluctance. Steve wasn't convinced that Sue was at fault, he thought that this went much deeper. How could the murderers have known that Harry was an undercover police officer? Still he now had another murder investigation on his hands, and it was still somehow linked to Manningsbrook Children's Home. Forensic recovery would be more difficult because the investigation was way behind, the scene was not secured, and the body had been taken away. This was unfortunate but it was nobody's fault, as no one in the station knew he was undercover. If they'd known it was a police officer, Steve knew for sure that the response would have been different. But the local police could not have been forewarned; with undercover operations it is vitally important that there is a sterile corridor, that information was given on a need-to-know basis only.

Steve decided to combine the two murder investigations, Harry and Aaron, because of the connection with the home. But why did Harry have to die? Was he getting close to something, or had he found something out but maybe hadn't realised its importance? He knew that Sue had tasked him to get close to Finn, was Finn key to this?

Sue had already arranged for a squad briefing that afternoon so when the team got together to update each other, there was a lot to talk about. Sue also invited the duty sergeant and Inspector Thorne to talk about their thoughts about Harry's death.

There were some interesting updates from outstanding actions. The action to trace and interview the previous long-term missing boy from the home, Jamie Simpson, was going nowhere. He had just disappeared from the home and was never seen again; surely this was suspicious?

Sean Moroney had been traced by two on-loan detectives to a flat near Swinton. The detectives had asked him about the argument that Luke had overheard between Jamie and Alan Rogers when he said he heard Jamie shouting about the Zodiac Club. Sean said that he did not remember such an incident and had never heard of the Zodiac Club, so this seemed like a dead end. Sean remembered that Jamie had seemed angry when he went missing but he had no idea what it was all about.

DS Paul Smith thought of a number of follow-up questions, which should have been asked, but none of them had occurred to the two detectives to ask Sean. *This was the problem with drafting in new staff*, thought Paul, *they don't always go that step further on their own initiative when needed.* It would probably be easier to go there himself.

According to the DVLA, there were ninety-six small white vans over ten years old registered at addresses within a twenty-mile radius. From the police computer they had identified five registered sex offenders who owned white vans in their area. They had all been interviewed and gave alibis which seemed to rule them out, but enquiries continued.

Chapter 26

Harry went to the door when the doorbell rang. He wasn't expecting to see anyone he knew because the flat was just a cover and none of his friends knew this address. He was surprised to see a senior police officer, whom he recognised immediately, at the door in plain clothes but smartly dressed in twill trousers and jacket. *Strangely*, thought Harry, *he was also wearing leather driving gloves.*

Harry looked puzzled. Although undercover, Harry answered instinctively, "Hello sir, can I help you?"

"Don't worry, I know what you're doing here. I wanted to see you to discuss something, I hope you don't mind, can I come in?"

Harry was worried and confused, "What, why, no, I don't mind, come in." Harry stepped aside to allow him to enter the sparsely furnished one-bedroomed flat, which was the converted ground floor of a small Victorian terraced house.

As they stood in the lounge, in awkward silence, the doorbell rang again. Harry excused himself, then went to open the door to two more men. One of them he had not seen before, but he was short and greasy. The other, he was surprised to see, was his manager, Alan Rogers.

Before he could ask why he was there, he felt a strong arm wrap around his neck from behind. He was dragged back into the flat, with his air supply cut off by the big man's forearm being squeezed across his windpipe. Harry realised that he must have crept up behind him and was now trying to strangle him. In panic, Harry managed to struggle free. He tried to run to the door, but the other men blocked his exit. They pulled him to the ground in a mass tumble then pinned him down.

"Taurus, Pisces! Hold his arms and legs, stop him struggling." said Capricorn.

Capricorn grabbed a cushion from the sofa then held it tight across Harry's face denying him vital air to breathe. They all held on tight, not allowing Harry any opportunity to struggle free. Harry's movements became slower and slower until they finally stopped completely.

The three then stepped away looking, at the now-deceased body of DC Harry Thomson whom Rogers had known as his newest staff member, Laurence Cook.

"Now we make this look like a suicide." Capricorn pulled out a sheet of paper which had been printed off at the children's home. It said just one word in bold capitals, "SORRY".

Taurus produced a rope from inside his jacket like a magician; it was already tied into a noose. Wearing gloves themselves they rubbed the noose knot and the rope roughly on Harry's hands, then put the noose over his head. They carried the body to the bedroom, looking around to find a suitable position from which to hang the young man. The bedroom had a built-in wardrobe with a robust-looking internal bar. Positioning a chair in front of the wardrobe and tying the rope to the bar, they sat Harry down, tightened the rope then pushed Harry off leaving him to hang in the wardrobe.

Taurus was worried; with all the deaths going on, things seemed to be getting out of control. Pisces, who had a very strong survival instinct, decided that it was time to head off on a holiday. There was nothing to link him to any crimes and it would not be smart to sit around waiting for evidence to surface. Luckily, he only leased the shop and flat on a short lease, so it would be easier to quickly disappear. After all he had no real ties, his cash was fluid, it was all going wrong here, so why not go to Spain or somewhere similar where he could hide away?

Capricorn was upbeat and whistling tunelessly as they went their separate ways away from their crime. By the time he reached home, though, he'd started to feel a bit uneasy. He poured himself a whisky and sat on his favourite chair. It was getting messy, it seemed like someone was targeting them, but he had no idea who and now, there was more killing. They'd had to do quite a bit of tidying up which was risky as they could be exposed.

Would the group keep it together, or would someone lose their nerve? His bet was on Pisces losing his nerve; he was a grubby little fellow, his only value to the group was supplying the flat above the shop. He looked like an unreliable type who would not hold up well under investigation or interview.

Chapter 27

I nearly wet myself when the police showed up at my flat. Thank God I had cleaned the bomb-making stuff away, if I hadn't, they'd have caught me. They didn't want to talk about the bombing, however. They said they were there to talk about Luke who had said that some time ago he had overheard an argument between Jamie and Alan Rogers. They asked if I'd heard Jamie shouting about the Zodiac Club or if I remembered the argument. I said that I did not remember such an incident and had never heard of the Zodiac Club. That seemed to satisfy them, but they said they'd be back if they had more questions.

I don't know why they came to me, they said that Luke had told them to, but do I believe them? I don't think I do; I think they're after me for the bombings. They can't be sure that it was me, or surely they'd have arrested me already. I need to step up my timetable before they stop me. Picking up my hit list I looked down and saw that the next name was Libra — councillor Roger Davies. He was a nasty old man, full of his own self- importance. He was single, lived alone in a flat in Leeston. He boasted about his influence and connections, implying that he was paid a lot of money for his influence. I didn't like that he was corrupt, or that he always wore too much aftershave and had a liking for inflicting pain.

With the police interested in me I had to step up my agenda so I could complete my mission. I would go for Libra tonight; I had six names on my list, and I needed to get moving on this. I pulled out my bomb-making stuff which I'd bought through the dark web, following instructions posted by Al Qaeda or someone like them. To be clear, I want you to understand, I am not a terrorist, I am an avenger, a hero, fighting evil.

I put my bomb together very carefully; I find that I am becoming quite adept at this and I am getting quicker. Soon I have my bomb ready and fit the cheap mobile phone which will detonate it. I will be targeting Libra tonight because he is fairly easy to watch as he parks his car in a quiet car park at the rear of his block of flats. There is a great vantage point to watch the car park without being caught on the hop, like with Aries.

As I am lost in thought I am disturbed by a firm knock at the door. I freeze; I'm not expecting anyone. A knock again — louder this time. I'm getting scared and stay very still. A knock again, this time the letterbox opens, and someone looks in, "It's the police, open up." I feel panic. Clutching my list, I try to think.

At the front of Sean Moroney's flat DS Paul Smith knocked firmly on the door. He could see a light inside and could hear movement when he lifted the letterbox before knocking. He waited a short time then knocked again.

Still no answer. Paul knocked again and opened the letterbox, shouting to open the door. There was still no answer, then suddenly there was a huge explosion emanating from the flat, blasting the front door off its hinges and throwing Paul to the ground, knocking him unconscious.

After a few minutes Paul came to and picked himself up, unhurt but dazed and confused; his head was buzzing as if he was lying at the bottom of a swimming pool. Paul then remembered where he was but still couldn't think clearly and couldn't hear anything but the buzz in his head. Paul stumbled into the flat through the gap where there had recently been a door. Should he do this, he wasn't thinking clearly, wasn't there something about secondary devices? Going in, he saw that the flat was small inside and its entire contents had been either devastated or flung around.

There was an unrecognisable body in the centre of the room, its body parts had been torn off and scattered across the room. In one corner Paul could see a forearm and a hand clutching a piece of paper. Curious, Paul pulled the piece of paper from the severed appendage. It had been a list of names but was now partially destroyed. It read:

<u>THE ZODIAC CLUB</u>
SCORPIO — PETER CALDER
ARIES — CLIVE OWEN
LIBRA — ROGER DAVIES
PISCES — DAVE FEN
TAURUS — ALA
CAPRICORN —

Frustratingly, the last three names were either partially or completely obliterated but Paul was amazed at what he was reading. This was like finding the Rosetta Stone, a key to deciphering this case! There were still so many questions: what does all this mean, are the bombings and the Aaron Wheeler murder connected? So, it seems there really is a Zodiac Club, but what are they about and whose are the missing names? Was Sean Moroney a victim of the bomber; if so, why?

While all these thoughts were running around his head his hearing returned with a rush of sound. He could hear the wailing of sirens and the sound of people shouting at him. With the explosion of sound Paul became confused and couldn't understand what was going on. Why were people shouting at him, he'd only come here to see someone to clear something up, but now he couldn't remember what?

An ambulance arrived and the paramedic shepherded Paul to the ambulance. Paul didn't want to go with them to the hospital, but they insisted and he didn't have any choice, it seemed. The fire service arrived next in a loud and furious barrage of activity. They made sure that the flat was not at risk of re-combusting but then withdrew quickly. The fire examiner had seen what looked like bomb-making equipment scattered around, and fearing further devices, sensibly cleared the vicinity, asking the police to manage the evacuation.

The police response car arrived and cordoned off the area, evacuating adjacent properties. A control centre was set up and the three services talked about next steps. A bomb disposal team had been called; they would need to make the flat safe before any forensics recovery started. Bomb disposal would take an hour to arrive so most activity ground to a halt. The police were interviewing residents, by going house to house but little was known about the flat or its occupant other than the consensus that it was a flat owned by social services and that a young man with a bicycle lived there. No one knew his name nor had ever spoken to him, but a description was given which sounded like Sean Moroney.

Paul Smith was taken to hospital in Swinton so had left the scene by the time DI Taylor had arrived to take charge. Once Sue had made sure everything was in place there, she decided to go and see her DS in hospital. She was naturally worried about Paul whom she considered not just a colleague but also a friend. Sue was thinking that there must be a connection with the explosion and the reason for Paul being there. She liked Paul a lot, but he was a bit of a maverick and she wasn't always aware of what he was doing.

When she arrived at the hospital, she talked her way into the ward where her DS was sitting up in bed drinking water. He looked pale and shaken but smiled thinly as Sue approached. "Hello boss."

"Having a nice rest, Paul?"

"Lovely," he coughed and grimaced with pain.

"What are the doctors saying?"

"A bit of concussion and bruised ribs. I'm still waiting for a CT scan. I'll be OK."

"It sounds like you were lucky."

"That's me… lucky."

"What were you doing there Paul?"

"Just following up on an action that needed more answers. Sean was a resident at the home when another boy went missing and was there when Luke first heard about the Zodiac Club. He'd denied it but it wasn't our own people who'd seen him. I thought he hadn't been pressed enough for information from what was a key period. I was there to quiz him a little bit closer."

"So, what happened?"

"I knocked the door and it exploded out on me. I don't know if it was an accident or what, but I found this." He handed Sue the Zodiac Club list. "I found it in his hand, it got damaged in the blast but it's very revealing."

Sue with her usual incisive brain immediately had a hypothesis about the meaning of the list. "So, it seems that Sean had been a resident at the home, knew about the Zodiac Club, had a grudge against these people and was blowing them up one by one."

"That's my thought as well."

"What would motivate someone enough to want to blow another person up?" asked Sue.

"Sexual abuse?"

"Maybe. So, is Aaron's murder linked to the bombings as well and, if so, we need to know why?"

"This scrap of paper is a huge step forward to finding out who, at least," mused Paul.

Chapter 28

DCI Steve Jones was sat in the office when his mobile rang. It was the professional standards department, the people who policed the police. The head of PSD explained that they had just taken a call from a furious Peter Calder who complained that the Family Liaison Officer assigned to his family following the bombing, had been having an affair with his wife, Naomi.

Steve shook his head in disbelief, then through gritted teeth promised to deal with the matter. Feeling angry he hung up the phone, Steve wondered what on earth the FLO, DC Nick Jeffers had been thinking. Steve ordered Nick Jeffers to come to the office immediately. Half an hour later a cocky, twenty-five-year-old Nick Jeffers sauntered into the office, saying, “Hi boss, what can I do for you?”

“Well you can tell me how your role as FLO for the Calder family is going, for a start.”

“Not bad boss, nice people, don’t know why anyone would have anything against them.”

“So, what do you see as your main responsibilities as FLO in this case?”

Being a smart arse, Nick quoted the manual verbatim, "Gather material from the family in a manner which contributes to the investigation; to inform, and facilitate care and support for the family, who are themselves victims, in a sensitive and compassionate manner in accordance with the needs of the investigation; to gain the confidence and trust of the family, thereby enhancing their contribution to the investigation."

Steve was seething, "So nowhere in that role description does it say that you should be shagging the victim's wife?"

The colour drained from Nick's face, "Well… I… er…"

"Well said… so I take it that you admit to having sexual relations with Mrs Calder?"

Nick looked stricken, all his confidence and bravado now evaporated.

Steve continued, "What you have been doing is not only undermining the investigation, you bring the force into disrepute and that amounts to gross misconduct. Now clear your stuff from here and go back to your home station, you'll hear more about this."

Nick was desperate, "What about Naomi, I need to tell her, her husband doesn't care, he hasn't touched her in years?"

"Just stay away; you've done enough harm already." Steve would happily let some misdemeanours pass but this was very damaging and he had zero tolerance.

Whilst at the hospital visiting Paul, Sue Taylor decided to call in and see the pathologist on duty, this time,

Dr Howe. She knew that Harry's post-mortem was scheduled for that afternoon, but she didn't have the courage to go to it, so she'd sent DC Jo James in her place. Then the explosion happened, and Paul was hurt so she'd forgotten about the PM until now.

As she walked into the hospital building, she saw Dr Howe coming along the corridor. The main hospital was large, bright and modern with long, wide, brightly lit corridors. The mortuary, however, was situated in the old, Victorian part of the hospital with narrow, gloomy corridors. Sue always thought it a little creepy so was happy to see Dr Howe. They knew each other quite well and greeted each other warmly.

Sue became serious, "So is it suicide?"

"You'd think so, but no, what happened was inflicted on him by someone."

"Are you saying someone hanged him?"

"Probably but strangulation wasn't the cause of death. He was hanged post-mortem to make it look like suicide; in fact, he was suffocated."

"What, how do you know?"

"There were orange fibres in his mouth and nose. Someone suffocated him with a cushion; he couldn't have done it himself."

"How do you know it was a cushion?"

"Dr Howe smiled, "Your very capable colleague, Jo, e-mailed the scene photographs to me. There is an orange cushion on the sofa which looks like the same colour as the fibres I found. She's getting the cushion recovered for forensic examination, but I am certain we'll find a match."

Sue felt a guilty sense of relief; it wasn't her fault after all. Steve was right, these events *must* all be connected and the link is the Zodiac Club. She thanked the pathologist and headed back to Leeston.

It was drizzling so she had to keep the hood up, but she still enjoyed the feeling of driving her powerful Mercedes. She thought about the list and what it could mean. Obviously, they knew Peter Calder and Clive Owen were both bombing victims but how were they connected? She knew of a local councillor called Roger Davies; could he be the one referred to? She had no thoughts who Dave Fen could be but could "Taurus — Ala" be Alan Rogers, the children's home manager? That would make sense and he would be a clear link to the home, but the list was incomplete, so how many were actually in this club? What had they done that would cause Sean to want to kill them? Physical abuse, sexual abuse, maybe both?

What motivates these men? It looks like they probably killed Aaron and Harry and there was another boy, Jamie, who went missing but was never found. Was he another murder victim?

A flash of insight came to her with a jolt. What was Detective Chief Superintendent Irvine's role in all of this? She remembered that it was him who filed the Jamie Simpson, missing person case; he had tried to stop her investigating Aaron's murder; he had tried to blame her for Harry's death and he had inexplicably known about Aaron being missing from the home even before she did. Could

Scotty Irvine be in the Zodiac Club, maybe *he* was Capricorn? She knew now that she needed to speak to Steve, it was all starting to make sense.

Chapter 29

Arriving at Leeston Station, Sue was pleased to see Steve's car was still in the car park. She rushed to her office, keen to share her news. As she entered her office, Steve was hanging up the phone.

"Good news on the bombing case," he said, "we have a fingerprint hit on a sandwich wrapper found in the cemetery. You'll never guess who it is."

"Sean Moroney," Sue said with a thin smile.

Steve looked like a child at Christmas who has had their toys taken away. "How did you know?"

Sue went on to explain what developments there had been, with Paul going to Sean Moroney's place then getting blown up. She showed him the Zodiac Club list and explained her rationale for her suspicions about Scotty.

Steve looked thoughtful, "We'll need to talk to him about this."

Sue felt bitterness and disappointment well up inside her; she had just expressed serious concerns about DCS Scotty Irvine and Steve wanted to just have a *chat* with him? Sue was so angry she was speechless.

Seeing her face, Steve realised what she was thinking, "You misunderstand; I think we'll need to formally interview him. I know his birthday is around Christmas because I've heard him moan about it... I accept that he could be Capricorn, although I don't think he is."

Sue felt guilty for doubting Steve's integrity, "Thank you for trusting me."

Then reality hit home for Sue. Scotty Irvine was the most senior detective in the force, this was serious stuff, she had to be certain or it would be professional suicide.

Sue was a little less bullish now, "Maybe we should try to get some more concrete evidence first, all we've got is circumstantial?"

Steve was decisive, "Good idea; thanks to the list, we have suspects, so let's get some surveillance going and see if we can make some connections between club members. This will need to be top secret, so just a few of us will know. Let's put a tail on Calder, Rogers and Davies, we can't justify following Scotty Irvine, but he is a person of interest in this enquiry. I'll need to tell the chief constable, though."

"OK, good plan, we will crack this case, I have a very good feeling about this."

Chapter 30

"Well gentlemen, things have become interesting," declared Capricorn.

"*Interesting?!* Are you insane? Someone just murdered Aries and tried to kill Scorpio," said Libra.

Scorpio looked outraged, "I nearly died, you don't know what that's like."

"True, but what *you* don't know is that the bomber blew himself up yesterday. Our worries are over, our demons are put to rest."

The surviving members of the Zodiac Club were meeting for the first time in a while at the flat. Following disuse, the flat looked and smelled even worse than usual and everyone but Capricorn looked anxious.

"What happened?"

"We're not sure whether he accidentally or deliberately blew himself up. The police were at his door, but they never got to speak to him, so he couldn't have told them anything about us."

"Who was the bomber?" asked Libra.

"Sean Moroney," said Capricorn, "a former friend of the club."

"I don't remember him." Scorpio looked puzzled.

"It was a few years ago, I think before your time. He's been very patient in his planning, it seems," said Capricorn. "The point is, he's now dead and the police are not linking his death to anything other than the previous bombings."

Taurus rather stupidly asked, "Why was he doing it?"

Capricorn looked at him for a short while like he was an unpleasant bug, then with a bitter smile, said, "I don't know, he was always a bit troublesome I remember, a bit surly, I think."

Taurus cut in, "He was OK really, he wasn't a bad lad."

"Well, in that case he's certainly changed since then, he's been trying to kill us all!" Libra said peevishly.

"As I said, that's now all behind us. Now that the dust has settled a bit, I think we should have another meeting. I suggest that next week would be good; Taurus can you tell Finn?"

"Next Wednesday is good timing, as Finn has already found us a new friend. He looks perfect," added Taurus.

"OK. I look forward to it. Go safely gentlemen."

Chapter 31

Sue and Steve had a dilemma. They had to arrange surveillance on Manningsbrook Children's Home, Alan Rogers, Peter Calder and Roger Davies, all the while keeping the most senior detective in the force out of the loop, because Sue thought that he was probably caught up in it all.

They had decided that they needed to go directly to the chief constable with their suspicions, otherwise there would be a real risk of compromise. When they saw him, he was anxious, Irvine was his own appointment, he had worked with him in the past and although he knew the man was irascible, he thought him sound. On top of that they were also requesting to follow a local councillor; not just that, he was the lead councillor for policing. This would be politically damaging should it all go wrong.

When he had calmed down and listened to their reasoning, he was convinced they had a right to be suspicious and reluctantly authorised a covert surveillance operation, which included following Detective Chief Superintendent Scotty Irvine.

It was agreed that they would start the following day, Monday, early doors at six a.m., with a five-thirty briefing.

Sue and Steve called in at the incident room on their way home. There were still a number of people working even though it was Sunday evening. Sue sent everyone home saying they could get a fresh start on Monday. That's exactly what Sue wanted, a fresh start on the enquiry with a good plan for where they were going.

As people started to get ready to leave, Sue asked Sally, her best analyst, to stay behind. "Sorry Sally, I need some intelligence briefing packs by tomorrow morning for a five-thirty briefing. Can you stay on and do them please?"

"Sure, what's it all about?"

"Top secret, I'm afraid, but I think you'll see why when you see the list of subjects." As she said this, Sue handed her a piece of paper with a list of names, three of which Sally immediately recognised.

"Shit," the analyst said, "no one important then?"

"You can see why it needs to be kept quiet?"

"Top cop, leading businessman and big politician, of course, explosive stuff. I'll get on with all the usual databases and get it on your desk tonight. Do you want urgent telephone analysis from all the subjects? That would take a bit longer."

"Get it started, I'll need an association chart to show how they're all connected as well."

"OK, when I get the phone data, I'll start one."

"If it's not too inconvenient could you possibly please deliver the intelligence reports to my flat?"

"All right, no problem." At this, Sally and Sue parted. Sally was keen to get on with the research.

Sue added, "Oh, and about tonight? I don't want any papers left around the station; this is all need-to-know only, I don't want any information to leak out."

Steve and Sue sat together in her office to prepare the operation orders for the surveillance teams. It was a long slog and after they were happy that they had everything in place for the morning, they went their separate ways. Knowing that they'd need to get an early night, neither suggesting that they should get together that night.

Sue got into her Mercedes and took a moment to think about Steve. It wasn't at all weird working with him, she thought. Actually, they worked very well together, but she was having nagging doubts about him. Particularly in relation to Irvine. On the other hand, she was really getting quite used to having him around. He was such a calming influence on her and the polar opposite to her highly strung ex-husband. Could she be falling for him? If so, what did he think of her? They'd not used the L word yet to each other: what if she did, would he run a mile?

She headed out of town knowing that the ferry would not be running, so she needed to drive out and round to the road bridge to get to her flat on the marina. She was glad of the drive as she loved to think in the car. She was excited now, they had genuine leads and she felt confident that they'd get a good result.

When she pulled into the car park, she didn't see James parked up at the far end. Sue parked her car in her reserved space then walked towards the door to her block of flats. As she got to the outside door, someone grabbed her arm from behind. She spun round ready to fight, then saw that it was her ex-husband, James.

"Let go of me!" snapped Sue, pulling away.

"Where's your boyfriend? Has he dumped you already? I can't say I blame him, best thing I did was getting rid of you."

Sue didn't know whether to be angrier at his misrepresentation of the past or the fact that he had turned up at her home and accosted her. She could smell alcohol on his breath.

"Are you drunk?" Sue asked.

"Are you going to invite me in?"

"No way, just piss off."

James glared at her aggressively, "I want a divorce."

"That makes two of us."

"I just want to make sure that you're not going to make up lies about me."

"I don't need to; the truth is enough. Don't worry, I won't tell everyone what an abusive bastard you are."

"You pushed me into it because you're so unreasonable. That, and you're so obsessed with work you had no time for me."

Sue was flabbergasted but decided to say nothing. "If that's all, I need to go now, I've got an early start."

James started to walk away, then turned around, "Remember, do not make trouble or you'll regret it." He had to have the last word and Sue was content to let him have it.

Sue opened the door with a feeling of relief and slumped against the inside of the door. She was horrified to see that she was shaking, and she hated this. How could he still have such an effect on her? She also hated the fact that she hadn't been able to stand up to James and report him for what he did to her.

She poured herself a large glass of red wine and slumped into the sofa. The phone rang, it was Steve, but she couldn't face talking to him now so she just rejected the call. She thought of the disappointment of her failed marriage, she had loved him so much in the early days. What had gone wrong… *was* it her fault like he'd said? Would she do the same to Steve? No, she refused to believe that it was her fault, she wouldn't buy into James' self-delusion. She was strong, she needed to stay strong.

Sue picked up the phone and dialled Steve's number, she was relieved when he answered. They made small talk for ten minutes, then both happily said goodnight knowing they'd see each other in a few hours to brief the surveillance teams.

Chapter 32

Owing to the sensitivity of the operation, the briefing for the surveillance teams was held in the local fire station situated half a mile from Leeston town centre. The car park was packed, and everyone made their way to the large training room on the first floor. Sue and Steve were already there ready to start at five-thirty a.m. Sally, as promised, had delivered the intelligence packages to Sue's flat just before midnight. They were very comprehensive, containing photos, family trees, association charts, known addresses, hobbies, habits, phone numbers. None of the three subjects, Calder, Rogers nor Davies were known associates but Calder and Davies were both Freemasons as was Scotty Irvine. They all attended the same lodge. Although he was not a direct subject of the surveillance, he may turn up if he really was a member of the Zodiac Club, so his information was included in the briefing packs.

As Sue started the briefing, people were inevitably shuffling through their papers. There were twenty surveillance officers in the room, lined up in theatre style rows of chairs. They were all alert and casually dressed. A murmur started when they realised Scotty Irvine's name was on the list. Sue thought it best to just tell them that he was a possible associate and that they might come across him during the surveillance. She stressed the importance of secrecy, telling them they were not to mention this operation, even to colleagues.

The teams were assigned their individual targets and the briefing split up with each team leader taking over. *Well here we go*, thought Sue, *this had better be a success or my reputation will be in tatters.* She shuddered to think what Irvine would do to her if he found out.

When the teams had left the room and it was quiet, Sue looked at Steve. "Well Steve, here goes."

"It will be fine; we've got some good leads here. And let's face it, it will be interesting interviewing Scotty," he laughed.

Sue couldn't help but smile, "True. Let's make our way to the office. We need to carry on as normal."

They staggered their arrival, with Sue arriving first. Sue saw Sally, the analyst, already at her desk. Does she never stop, thought Sue? She wandered over to say thanks again for last night, but as soon as Sally spotted Sue, her eyes lit up. "We've got a possible lead on the van."

"Go on," said Sue.

"I've been going through the list of registered keepers and comparing it to the list of Zodiac members. We have Dave Fen as Pisces and we have a white 2002 plated, Ford Escort van registered to a David Fenwick of the "Happy Chippy" fish-and-chip shop, Hazel Road, Leeston. Get it?"

Sue got it, a fish-and-chip shop run by someone with the code name "Pisces", funny man. "What do we know about him?"

"Not a lot, he's been there a while. He's a frequent complainer about youth nuisance outside the small parade of shops; I think he's got the ear of the local police inspector, who is monitoring what is happening."

"Jon Thorne?"

"Yes, it seems he'll only speak to the inspector."

"Right, let's keep this development to ourselves for now. We haven't got enough people to follow him but let's set up an observation post to watch for any comings and goings. I'll also tell the surveillance team to be aware of the chip shop in case our subjects go there."

Sue thanked Sally again and headed towards her office just as Steve arrived. They both got coffee then sat together to talk.

"The bomber enquiry is officially over because of the death of Sean Moroney," started Steve, "but in truth we'll merge the two investigations together. Who can we trust to run the enquiries in total secrecy?"

"DS Paul Smith, of course, he can pick his own team of two DCs who are trustworthy to be in on the secret also. Thank goodness he's recovered from the blast and insists on coming back to work."

"So, what is this all about, do you think?" asked Steve.

Sue paused to marshal her thoughts before replying, "I am convinced we're on to a paedophile ring called the Zodiac Club. I think it stems out of the children's home, facilitated by the manager, Alan Rogers, who procures boys from the home for the group." She paused. "I suspect that Finn is involved somehow, maybe to help procure victims. A former victim, Sean Moroney, tried to kill Peter Calder and killed Clive Owen. Moroney then blew himself up when Paul Smith went to see him. We have an incomplete list of the members, but they all seem to be people with some influence." Sue hesitated, then carried on. "There is a possibility that Scotty Irvine is a member; he might be Capricorn, as he seems to know things about these events before anyone should. For some reason the club murdered Aaron, having plied him with drink and drugs. Jamie disappeared because he threatened them, and they murdered Harry because he was exposed as an undercover officer by Scotty Irvine."

Steve thought through what Sue had just said, "It all sounds so far-fetched, but I think you're right. All the evidence points to it being true and it looks like it's been going on for quite a while, but that just doesn't seem possible."

"With the children's home they have the perfect victims in the perfect environment. No one would believe them if they complained and the very person who poses the greatest risk to them is the one charged with their care."

"I see your point," said Steve, "it's a nice set-up really. But we're on to them now."

Sue looked serious, "I can't wait to take these bastards down, but we've still got to get the evidence first."

Chapter 33

The surveillance was going well, but the teams had made no progress in gathering evidence. Calder was up early and left for the office in his new BMW, which had replaced his bombed-out car. He left at seven-thirty a.m. and drove straight to his plastic container factory on a small industrial estate set in a farm about fifteen minutes from home. He stayed there all morning only leaving for lunch at the closest pub, The Royal Oak. According to its website, The Royal Oak is a quiet, thatched rural pub set in the Leeston Forest National Park. The emphasis is on real ales and good simple food. They welcome dogs and children, have a large garden and the pub features in CAMRA's 'Good Beer' guide. Calder didn't meet anyone there and had one pint while chatting to the landlord. After his beer he left and went straight back to the factory where he stayed until it was closed at six p.m. There were a number of visitors to the factory, but none seemed to be of any interest.

The surveillance team worked hard to monitor his activity, and at the end of the day they followed him home. The day was typical of surveillance, containing ninety percent boredom followed by moments of activity. When it was clear he wasn't going anywhere they stood down, frustrated, at about ten p.m.

Roger Davies was more exciting to follow as it turned out that he moved around a lot. As a local councillor, he spent quite a bit of time at the town hall but most of his time meeting people all over Leeston. He was on foot all the time and buzzed around furiously; this presented a far greater challenge for the surveillance team, who had to be on their toes all the time. He would typically turn up at a house or business, have a ten-minute chat, then scuttle away quickly. They guessed he was canvassing because of the upcoming local elections. If hard work guaranteed success, then he would certainly deserve to win.

There was nothing suspicious about any of his contacts, he even met the local police inspector in the station but had no meetings with any of the operation subjects.

Observations on the children's home yielded as little useful information. They observed children coming and going and the occasional glimpse of a care-worker but there was no sign of Alan Rogers after he arrived at work. The team sat patiently, waiting for movement all day, only occasionally breaking off for natural breaks and to stock up on food. After a fruitless day, the team stood down having followed him home at seven p.m., then waited another hour before giving up for the day.

The surveillance on the "Happy Chippy" fish-and-chip shop was more interesting. Firstly, Dave Fenwick was seen several times going up to a flat above the shops. This was interesting because the flat looked unoccupied and Fenwick was registered as living elsewhere. Looking through records, flat 4 was linked to the fish-and-chip shop and they were leased together.

Secondly, Fenwick was followed going to the local travel agent in the High Street, David Walker Travel, and was clearly planning a trip. The surveillance officer who went into the travel agent pretended to be a customer and was able to overhear him say that he wanted to leave for Spain as soon as possible. There was discussion about where to go and Fenwick was heard to say that he was actually thinking of moving to Spain and he wanted to live in an expat community. They discussed options at length, the agent talked knowledgably about the pros and cons of various regions, but finally settled on Alicante on the Costa Blanca. Fenwick booked a flight, leaving in two days' time, direct to Alicante.

Despite the interesting information about Pisces, Dave Fenwick, apparently fleeing the town, Sue was bitterly disappointed at the lack of progress. She complained to Steve over dinner in her flat, his only response being, "It will be better tomorrow."

Tuesday had to be a better day.

Meanwhile Capricorn was getting busy. He had contacted Zodiac Club members on the darknet to prepare for Wednesday. They communicated between each other on the darknet because their messages were untraceable, not leaving any footprint on the internet. They also used unregistered, pay-as-you-go mobile phones which were frequently changed. These were safe and reliable methods.

Everyone confirmed that they would come on Wednesday at one p.m. Taurus confirmed that Finn would bring the new boy and Pisces said that the flat would be ready, he had cleaned up a bit and, more importantly, they had enough drink and drugs in stock.

Chapter 34

It was late Tuesday afternoon and Finn was sitting in the lounge with his new best friend, Simon. "Hey, Simon, the good news is that you and I are going to a party tomorrow."

Simon's eyes lit up. "A party, where?"

"Nearby."

"Whose party is it?"

"Some friends, you don't know them, but it will be great," said Finn enthusiastically. "The thing is that it's in the afternoon, so you'll have to bunk off school."

Simon looked dismayed, "I can't bunk off, I'll get in trouble."

Finn's eyes narrowed, "You've got to, you've gotta go to the party."

"But I can't bunk off."

Finn looked threateningly at Simon and moved closer to him, "You have no choice, you've taken the money and stuff, so you owe me. You go to the party or you'll be in big trouble."

"Wh… what do you mean?" his eyes grew big.

"You don't want to find out."

Simon looked scared, "I thought you were my friend."

"I am, but I won't be if you let me down."

"All right, I'll come."

"Great, bunk off. I'll pick you up at lunchtime, we'll go together."

Finn left Simon on the sofa and went to see Alan Rogers in his office. He was on the phone as Finn knocked lightly, Alan waved for him to come in and sit down.

Finn sat down as Alan wrapped up his conversation then said, "Hello Finn, how are you?"

Finn tried to look nonchalant, "It's all good, I've had to lean on Simon a bit but it's all fine now."

"He will be there tomorrow, won't he? You know you can't let us down."

Finn looked worried. "He'll be there, I guarantee it."

Alan looked relaxed but there was a glint of malice in his eyes. "Well that's all right then isn't it?"

Finn looked down at his own feet.

"Well that's all right then isn't it?" repeated Alan viciously, striking Finn over the head for emphasis.

Finn's eyes welled up with the humiliation. He kept his eyes low and mumbled, "Yes, it'll be all right, I'll make sure of it, OK?"

"Good, now go and be nice."

Finn left, but didn't feel like being nice. He stormed out of the office, straight through the lounge, then the kitchen and out the back door. He strode across the lawn towards the High Street even though most of the shops were shut.

His mind was a whirl of emotions and thoughts. All at once he was frightened, angry, ashamed and excited. He hated being used but it gave him power over others. He strode quickly down the High Street until he neared the town hall. The building was red brick, Victorian and very attractive with large sweeping arched windows and an impressive entrance. What interested Finn, though, wasn't the architecture, it was the fact that he knew that Libra worked there. That and the hatred he felt when he thought of the look on Libra's face the night Aaron died.

As he walked past the building, he picked up a small rock and threw it at one of the smaller side office windows; even so it smashed dramatically on impact.

In truth, Finn didn't really know what he was thinking at the time he threw the rock. He just had the hatred and some vague notion that he wanted to get them back somehow. He was shocked to see a policeman come around the corner just after the window broke. The uniformed copper quickly realised what had happened and headed towards Finn.

Finn turned and started to run, but the copper shouted. "No point running Finn, I know who you are."

Finn stopped in his tracks; he knew he'd be in trouble but for some reason he felt OK by it. He stood still while the officer walked up to him, taking his time. Finn recognised him as a quite young policeman he'd met at the home before, probably when he'd been in trouble or had gone missing, as he used to do quite often. He remembered that he'd been kind before and thought maybe he'd go easy on him now.

"Did you just break that window?" the young policeman asked.

"No, it wasn't me, a young kid did it and just ran off." Finn went into his reflex mode of "auto-denial".

"What did this kid look like?"

"Dunno, small, blonde hair, I didn't get a good look."

"Do you know him?"

"No, he's probably a local kid."

The policeman looked at him seriously, then shook his head, "OK, I'm not sure I believe you but, the inspector has said we're to tell him first if you lot do anything stupid, so I'm not taking you in… *yet*."

The young policeman didn't feel quite comfortable about letting Finn go, but didn't have the courage to defy a senior officer's instruction. For his part, Finn thought, there were definitely some advantages to having friends in high places.

"Just remember, you need to stay out of trouble and if I find out it was you that broke the window, then we'll be seeing each other again," the copper said finally, then hurriedly headed towards the town hall to take a report about the damage.

Finn wandered slowly back to the home. As he was walking up the driveway, he saw Simon looking anxiously out of the front window. When Simon saw Finn, his face lit up and he rushed to the front door.

Finn laughed, "Hey kid, slow down, you'll blow a gasket." This was something his mother used to say, although he had no idea what a gasket was.

Simon couldn't contain himself. "I thought you were angry with me," he blurted, "I didn't think you were coming back. I'm sorry, I'll go to the party, I'll bunk off like you said."

Finn looked more resigned than happy, but managed a weak smile, "That's all right then."

Chapter 35

The surveillance started early Tuesday but was another washout. Yet again the surveillance teams watched their respective subjects go about their daily routines with nothing suspicious to report. All phone data had been gathered but there was nothing to link any of them. However, if they had any sense, they'd use unregistered mobile phones, to avoid being tracked.

As evening drew in, Scotty Irvine turned up unexpectedly in DI Taylor's office. She looked up and flushed as he sat down heavily in a spare chair. His complexion was usually florid due to heavy drinking, but on this occasion his face was livid.

"You're having me followed?" he asked, but it was more of a statement than a question.

Sue answered truthfully, "No we're not."

"Don't get fucking clever with me, little girl, I know you referred to me in a surveillance briefing, which, by the way, I didn't authorise and know nothing about. And why are you on a case I've already taken you off?"

Sue didn't know what to say. So much for a sterile corridor for intelligence! Who had leaked this operation to

Irvine? One of his boys' club, no doubt. Sue was suddenly angry; she'd done nothing wrong. "The chief constable authorised the operation."

"But at your request? You evil bitch, no wonder your husband left you," he said spitefully.

Sue calmed down a bit. "Look, you know I can't talk to you about this."

Now he was shouting at her. "You've got a fucking cheek. I will get you for this, you don't want me as an enemy! Anyway, I've pulled the surveillance team off for some *real* work, a counter-terrorism job, not your insane imaginings borne of malice. So, your stupid nonsense stops now."

With this he stormed out and an uncomfortable silence spread across the squad room. No one wanted to meet Sue's gaze. Sue was flushed with impotent anger and glared at Steve as he walked in, not knowing what had just passed and what he was now in for.

Sue and Steve sat down without a word, Sue was shaking with fury but managed to say, "Some bastard leaked to Scotty that we were doing surveillance, he just came here and bawled me out."

"That's not really surprising, he's got a lot of allies, you know that."

"He's pulled the operation, we're stuck."

Steve looked shocked, "He can't do that, that's going against the chief constable's authority. Don't worry I'll have a word, but I think we'll need to talk to Scotty, sooner rather than later."

"Good, I'll get him arrested."

"No, we'll invite him in, but I'll tell the chief constable first."

Following a fractious telephone call with the chief constable, Steve phoned Irvine. The chief had agreed with his assessment and accepted that they had to interview Irvine. The corruption unit would be on stand-by, depending on how the interview went.

"Scotty, it's Steve."

"Hi Steve, how can I help you?"

"Look, this is awkward, but I need to talk to you formally about what's going on."

Irvine sounded more shocked than angry. "Are you arresting me, Steve?"

"No, but there are questions we need to ask."

Now Irvine sounded angry, "We? You mean you and that bitch? I will not be interviewed by her, just you. I don't trust her."

"Do you trust me?"

"You know I do."

"And you also know you can't say who does or doesn't interview you. Sue is a great detective and knows more about this case than anybody. She needs to be in on the interview."

For a while Irvine said nothing, then with a sigh, "When and where? Will I need a lawyer?"

"Can you be at Leeston, say at eleven-thirty a.m.? It's up to you whether you need a lawyer."

"What's it all about?"

"Manningsbrook Children's Home, specifically, two boys who went missing from there, Jamie Simpson, who has never been found and Aaron Wheeler, who was found murdered recently." Steve deliberately held back their concerns about Harry's death.

"OK." Irvine abruptly hung up the phone.

Sue was watching on anxiously, "I heard what you said, thanks for sticking up for me, Steve."

"I meant what I said but I *am* sticking my neck way out for you."

Sue spontaneously hugged him, causing them both to laugh with relief. "That could have gone a whole lot worse," said Steve.

"Let's see what happens when he comes in. We've got a couple of hours, let's get coffee and review what we've got to ask him."

They decided to go to the local coffee shop to try to relax. With the surveillance cancelled and with everyone else already tasked with investigations they had a bit of spare time on their hands. They sat on a comfortable sofa after ordering their drinks.

Steve sighed and Sue asked, "What are you thinking?"

"Well I know we've got to question him, but I do hope he's innocent; I've worked with him, he's a good man."

"Are you kidding me? That bastard would love for a chance to get at me. He's a dinosaur and a raging misogynist."

"But that doesn't necessarily make him a criminal."

Chapter 36

While Sue and Steve were making their plans, Alan Scotty Irvine was making his own. He had no intention of just lying down and rolling over. He still thought that Sue had it in for him and he wasn't minded to let her get away with it. But first he had a few things to do; luckily, he had an idea of where to start.

Knocking on the door of Jon Thorne's flat in Leeston, Irvine was worried and puzzled. Inspector Jon Thorne was a fellow Freemason and had been his spy in Leeston police station for many years. Thorne was a solid chap and had his finger on the pulse of everything going on, he'd know what this was all about. Irvine kept on top of things around the force by cultivating loyal spies in each locality; not all were Freemasons, but they were all trustworthy, at least he thought so. Now he wasn't so sure about Steve Jones, he must have been contaminated by that Taylor woman.

He thought about what he knew. Some years ago, he'd made a cock-up. He'd been asked by Jon Thorne to write off a missing persons enquiry because it was a bit embarrassing for the force's lack of progress. In fact, no efforts had been made to track the individual down.

Everyone knew that the boy had gone home but there was no proof. Slightly against his better judgement, he had agreed to do it, why was this a problem now?

Of more concern was the recent death of the little boy, Aaron Wheeler. On the day in question, Jon Thorne had phoned him early to tell him what was going on. He'd mentioned the missing boy, that he had gone missing overnight and had probably died of hypothermia whilst out sleeping rough. He had explained that it wasn't out of character and there was nothing suspicious about the death.

He'd taken Jon Thorne at his word, so it wasn't his fault that Taylor's sources of information were slower than his. He was however, concerned that Jon Thorne was a little too quick about wanting to write it off as non-suspicious. Being the children's home liaison inspector, he would know more than anyone else about the residents. He wasn't to know what the post-mortem would find, but that was a little embarrassing. How did she manage to do this, how did she get under his skin? It wasn't that he hated women; in fact, in his younger years, he had a lot of success with women. He liked women but she shouldn't be a detective inspector, in his opinion. She was too emotional, too irrational. What he wanted was a more reliable, solid chap in post; Sue Taylor was an irritation he wanted to get rid of.

While Chief Superintendent Irvine was contemplating Sue and his next move, her office phone rang. Sue was alone in her office when she answered, it was the switchboard, “Do you want to take a call from Jade from Manningsbrook Children’s Home?”

“Yes, put her on.”

Chapter 37

Jade was sitting curled up dozing on a large, comfortable armchair in the corner of the lounge at the children's home. Also sitting in the lounge was the new boy, Simon. He was fidgeting, seeming to be waiting for something or someone. She didn't speak to him, she just didn't, that just doesn't happen, ever.

When Finn breezed into the room, full of cheer, Jade thought it sounded forced and false. "Hey, little dude, time for us to go party." Finn couldn't see her, and when she realised that she wasn't visible to him, Jade decided to keep quiet and stay down to see what would happen.

"OK." Simon seemed a bit nervous and didn't move.

"Come on big fella, it's time for us to go, we've got Zodiac Club, it's going to be a laugh."

Jade almost jumped at the words Zodiac Club but stayed down instead, curling herself tighter to make sure she could not be seen.

Simon got up slowly, seemingly in two minds.

"Come on slow coach, we've got to get going."

The two then walked out the back way via the kitchen. Jade quickly decided to follow them and get to the bottom of the Zodiac Club mystery. She ran to the back door just in time to see them turn left out of the gates. She lost sight of them as she ran across the garden towards the road. Jade stopped at the gate and peered carefully around the corner. She could see them walking along the pavement about fifty metres ahead. She waited a second then followed them out. She walked close to the hedges to avoid being seen and managed to keep them in sight until they turned into the "Trees" estate. She saw them turn into Hazel Road but by the time she'd reached the junction they were out of view, she'd lost them.

"Shit," she muttered under her breath as she turned around to walk back to the home, wondering what she should do. Then she thought of the nice lady detective she'd met, was it DC Janes or James? Her first name was Jo, she remembered.

When she was alone in her room, she took out her phone and called the police. She was answered by a call handler. Jade was almost put off speaking but instead said, "I'm calling about Aaron Wheeler's murder, can I speak to someone? Is DC James there?"

After a short while the operator said, "Sorry, DC James is on a rest day today, can anyone else help?"

Jade, not to be deterred said, "I think it's important, can I speak to whoever is in charge?"

"That might not be possible, I'll try the incident room."

By good fortune, during the lunch break Sue would have calls forwarded to her office phone, so that no calls were missed. This was unusual for a senior officer, and another reason for her staff to value her as a boss who wasn't afraid of work.

Sue answered her phone, it was the switchboard, "Do you want to take a call from Jade from Manningsbrook Children's Home?"

"Yes, put her on..." There was a click and she said, "DI Taylor, how can I help?"

"My name is Jade Matheson, I'm from Manningsbrook Children's Home. I think you may be interested in the Zodiac Club?"

Sue sat up suddenly on high alert. "What do you know about it?"

"I know Finn just took the new boy, Simon, there. I overheard them talking and Finn said that he was taking Simon to a party at the Zodiac Club. I'll be honest, the way he said it creeped me out."

"So where is this club?"

"I'm sorry, I don't know. I tried following them when they left but I lost them in the "Trees" estate."

"Where exactly?"

"They turned into Hazel Road but I lost sight of them, so I don't know where they went after that."

Sue had a flash of inspiration, "Could they have gone into the shops?"

"I don't know, I suppose so, I couldn't see."

"Well, Jade, you did the right thing by calling, we'll get right on it. Another thing, if they come back or you find anything else out, call me straight away." Sue gave Jade her mobile number then hung up.

Her next call was to Paul Smith, who was out of the office. "Paul, I need you here now with house entry team. Finn has taken a young boy, Simon, from the care home to the Zodiac Club. They were heading for the Trees estate; I need someone to urgently check the Hazel Road shopping precinct CCTV to see where they go."

"I'm on it," said Paul. That was one of the reasons why she liked Paul; no unnecessary questions, just action. She was so grateful he was back at work. Within ten minutes, people were filing into the squad room with a buzz of excitement, waiting for instruction. Paul phoned her back with the news that the CCTV operator saw a boy matching Finn's description, he had been seen going around to the rear of the shops with a smaller boy about half an hour ago.

I bet they are in the flat above the fish-and-chip shop, Sue thought, which would make sense and would tie in with Dave Fenwick being a member of the Zodiac Club. They could well be using the flat for their activities.

Chapter 38

Sue called the team together into the squad room and gave a short briefing. The group quietened down as she came into the room, everyone eager for news. She outlined the background of the investigation so that they were up to speed and then told them of her suspicions that there was a paedophile ring called the Zodiac Club operating out of the flat. She pointed out that they were dangerous men, probably responsible for at least one murder. She said that Chief Superintendent Irvine might be there and was to be arrested for child abuse and murder, along with anyone else they might find at the location.

Meanwhile Paul Smith had been frantically writing instructions, allocating people to teams and dividing tasks such as entry, arrest and search teams. Rather than taking time to get a warrant to enter the flat they were going in using PACE (Police and Criminal Evidence) Act powers of entry in order to arrest the people they found.

As soon as everyone was ready and had been allocated tasks, the fifteen detectives and uniformed officers made their way to their vehicles in the rear yard. Everyone looked grim and serious as they filed out of the back door of the station; even so, they were excited at the prospect of some serious action.

Sue went in a car with Paul and suddenly remembered that Steve did not know what they were doing. As she sat in the front passenger seat, she pulled out her phone to dial his number. It went to answerphone, so she left a brief message. Part of her was relieved because she still felt that he was loyal to Irvine and she didn't want any awkwardness. She pushed that to the back of her mind and concentrated on the operation.

Unlike TV programmes, the convoy of police cars did not roar off in a cacophony of flashing blue lights and sirens, which would only alert the perpetrators. Instead they drove off briskly, but quietly, in convoy, arriving at their destination some five minutes later. As instructed, all the vehicles parked out of sight of the flats above the shops. The officers all then jogged in single file round to the rear of the shops. They kept close to the fences, taking advantage of natural cover. Two remained at the front of the shops with a view of the windows in case there were attempts to leave or dispose of evidence.

The rest quietly made their way up the iron stairway onto the concrete walkway. As they neared the flat, they could hear muted music. The entry team, wearing paramilitary clothing, stepped forward with the large door ram and, protected by thick armoured gloves, they immediately smashed the flimsy UPVC door in, knocking it completely off its hinges.

There was shouting as the arrest teams, similarly dressed, streamed past the entry team, several of whom had body worn video cameras. What they saw shocked even the most hardened, experienced officers.

In the middle of the lounge were some men, naked from the waist down and all with cameras slung around their necks. Knelt down in the middle of this bizarre group was a thin, naked boy covered in oil wearing a dog collar and leash. He was swaying rhythmically to the music, oblivious to anything around him. One officer stepped in and bundled the boy up in his large police jacket. The boy said nothing.

As the police burst in, they saw the door at the other side of the room close, as if someone had just slipped out. A couple of officers went through the door and, sure enough came back a few minutes later, with someone dressed in a forensic suit.

The other men were quickly handcuffed, then dressed in white forensic over-suits also. They all sat on the grubby sofa, their heads hanging down staring at a fixed spot on the carpet ahead of themselves. None of them had said anything since their initial protests when the police broke in.

Now that the scene was secured Sue entered and took control, "Right, I want everything forensically seized in situ, including those four." She nodded towards the Zodiac Club. "Take Simon to the sexual assault referral centre, go gentle."

Sue was curious, Scotty Irvine wasn't there, she didn't know whether she felt disappointment or relief. So, who was the unknown club member? Even with their heads bowed she could recognise Calder, Davies and Rogers but Fenwick wasn't there, so who was the fourth man?

Walking over to the sofa she felt uneasy as she realised that she recognised him. "Hello Inspector Thorne," she said flatly. She couldn't believe her own eyes; the last member, Capricorn, was Inspector Jon Thorne.

Thorne said nothing but his shoulders shook slightly, and he looked up with mortification and fear etched on his face. Sue felt no sympathy for him; these people were paedophiles and murderers.

Finn was sat apart from the others, Sue walked towards him. His head was bowed like the others, but he was crying with huge racking sobs. He spoke between his tears, "I didn't want any of this, they made me do it, I'll tell you everything you want to know." He was pointing at the Zodiac Club members without looking up.

Sue just shook her head in disgust at all of them, she couldn't get the image of what was going on out of her mind. They must have done the same, and more, to Aaron. She then had a thought. "Where's Fenwick?" she said aloud to no one in particular.

Councillor Roger Davies, seeing an opportunity to ingratiate himself said, "We haven't seen that weasel all day, I think he's making his escape, it's his flat you know."

Thorne rounded on him, "Shut your mouth, say nothing."

"Just get them out of here," Sue instructed.

Finn was a different matter entirely; when the police raided the flat, he broke apart. Finn was terrified, he knew the game was up, he tried to curl up and hide on the chair, he just wished it would swallow him up. All he wanted to do was tell the police everything and minimise his own involvement.

While the men were all handcuffed, Finn was being comforted by an officer as if he had been assaulted. He was told by a friendly, young policewoman that he'd have to make a statement but there was no rush, they could do it tomorrow since he was clearly traumatised. Finn couldn't believe his luck until the senior detective in charge saw him and said, "Constable, he's to be arrested as well. Don't fall for the tears, he's in it up to his neck."

The officer looked upset, "OK, ma'am. Sorry, I thought he was a victim."

"He may well be, but we know that he brought Simon from the home to this place today, so he's got some tricky questions to answer. We'll start by treating him as a suspect then go from there. Besides he lied to us about not knowing about the club."

When they got back to the station, Sue met up with Steve. "Sorry I couldn't get hold of you to join in on the bust."

"My fault, I was looking for Irvine, it was a waste of time, he's disappeared. In any case this has always been your job, I've formally handed the investigation to you, as you are the senior investigating officer leading the case."

"No problem, we've got enough to be doing with the ones arrested at the flat. You'll never guess who we *did* find there, though, Jon Thorne."

"Thorne, the Leeston inspector?" Steve asked incredulously.

Sue was deep in thought, "Yep, I think he's Capricorn. He was the leak all along, he must have been feeding misinformation to Irvine."

"And Irvine trusted him over you. He's obviously got a guilty conscience if he's avoiding us."

With impeccable timing, Chief Superintendent Irvine walked into the room, "Who's been avoiding us Steve?"

Steve recovered quickly, "Fenwick from the Zodiac Club, he's on the run. You ready for a chat?"

"That's why I'm here, let's get on with it."

Their conversation was surprisingly cordial. Irvine and Sue were cool but professional. Irvine confirmed that his information source was Inspector Jon Thorne. He even admitted that he had made an error of judgement about him and may have misjudged Sue because of this. It seems that Thorne had been feeding Irvine misinformation about Sue, making it look like she was incompetent and disloyal. All the while Thorne was manipulating things to protect the Zodiac Club.

Sue and Irvine ended the interview on good terms, even shaking hands at the end. To be honest it wasn't exactly a love in, but it was a start.

When Irvine had left, Steve smiled at Sue, "That's a good day's work. The whole club has been captured bang to rights apart from Fenwick."

"I've been thinking about that, I think I know where he's going."

Sue got Paul in and they discussed next steps. "Do you remember during surveillance that Fenwick went to a travel agent? Get someone there and find out if he's booked to leave, I seem to remember he was interested in Spain, let's wreck his holiday plans."

Chapter 39

Heathrow airport was its usual crazy, busy environment. Filled with hope and expectation, passengers queued with seemingly infinite patience which was akin to the fortitude of Hercules before they could board their plane.

Dave Fenwick, Pisces, formerly of the Zodiac Club, was waiting for his flight to Alicante and a new life. He was waiting at gate sixteen for his plane, scheduled to leave in just fifteen minutes. Fenwick felt excited and elated. He congratulated himself on his foresight; he had a feeling it was all going wrong, which is why he fled without telling anyone. The others were fools. They were so arrogant and self-confident, they treated him like a fool, but who was the fool now?

As he was driving to the airport, he'd had a call from a neighbour asking him why the police were raiding his flat. The neighbour had seen the police go in, then later come out with some men in white overalls and handcuffs. He wanted to know why but Fenwick was no help, so he gave up, promising to keep an eye out. Fenwick switched his phone off.

At the airport Fenwick repeatedly checked his ticket and passport, willing the minutes to pass. When everyone was called forward to board he lined up with the rest of the passengers towards the front of the queue. As he arrived at the desk he was smiling as he held out his boarding pass and passport. The woman behind the desk looked past him and nodded and, as if from nowhere, two burly men in suits stepped up beside him.

"Step out of the line please sir," said one.

"But I'll miss my flight," pleaded Fenwick.

"You won't be flying today sir, you're under arrest for child abuse and murder, I don't think you'll be flying for quite a while," said the second drily.

Fenwick's legs gave way and the two policemen had to prop him up to stop him collapsing to the ground. He felt sick and dizzy as they walked him unceremoniously to the airport's holding area. Fenwick tried to protest his innocence but quickly gave up when it was obvious that they didn't know anything, they were just there to transport him. So, Fenwick gave up talking and started thinking; how quickly could he give the rest of the Zodiac Club up for his own advantage? Fenwick was a cockroach; he'd heard that they can survive nuclear war. He would survive this, he was sure.

Having put Paul in charge of the interviews, Sue thought they went well. Peter Calder, Roger Davies and David Fenwick couldn't confess fast enough to their involvement in the club, although they denied murdering Aaron or Harry. All three claimed to have a minimal role in the club, it being principally run by Alan Rogers and Jon Thorne.

Neither Jon Thorne nor Alan Rogers said much during their interviews; Thorne just kept repeating no comment to every question asked. Rogers only spoke about his role as manager and carer at the children's home, completely failing to see the contradiction between his job to keep vulnerable kids safe and his actions by procuring and abusing the very young boys he should have been protecting.

Sue wasn't too bothered about what they actually had to say about the sexual abuse as they had evidence aplenty. Sue decided to treat Finn as a victim and witness because his involvement started as a victim of the club and he was clearly coerced to help them when he became too old for their tastes. He made an extremely comprehensive video-recorded interview detailing what had been done to him and what he'd been forced to help them do to other boys. This included a graphic account of that terrible night when Aaron died; he described the awful sight of his dying moments and how he had put the clothes back on Aaron over the stench of vomit, faeces and blood.

After several days in custody, the Zodiac Club members were all charged with the sexual abuse of children and the murder of Aaron. With only circumstantial evidence connecting any of them to the murder of Harry, no one was charged with his murder. Sue was still convinced that there was a connection and would keep trying to prove it.

Chapter 40

After this, Sue and Steve's relationship got into a comfortable and steady pace. They still saw each other regularly and Steve stayed over whenever possible. They were both busy people so had little spare time and didn't see each other as much as they would have liked.

A month later Steve got a promotion to detective superintendent, while Sue was overlooked again. Sue thought that although she had reconciled things with Irvine, her stock had fallen with the chief constable for raising him as a suspect during the Zodiac investigation. Sue also heard that there was criticism of her for not spotting Jon Thorne's involvement. She felt she truly could not win.

As the trial approached, Sue had left the file building to one of her aspiring detective sergeants, Jo James. Jo had been successful at the recent promotion board and was glad to remain part of Sue's team. Jo's relationship with Paul was moving at a spectacularly slow rate. They met and had dinner every couple of weeks, but had hardly moved on at all. She wondered whether Paul was really interested in her or not but was afraid to ask the question.

Sue was sitting in her office with Jo going over the Zodiac file when she took an uncharacteristically terse call from Damian Johnson, the head of the local crown prosecution service, the lawyers responsible for prosecuting cases at court.

"I need to talk to you urgently," Damian said with no preliminaries or pleasantries.

"Why?" Sue was puzzled as they normally got on well.

"My office tomorrow, eight-thirty a.m." He just hung up, not waiting for Sue to agree.

"What was all that about?" asked Jo.

Sue was thoughtful. "I don't know but I don't like the sound of it."

Sue realised she had been right to be worried when she was sitting in Damian's office the following morning. He swept in and started in on her, "DI Taylor I am frankly disappointed in you. How did you think you'd get away with it? You know we'll all look stupid dropping charges against him. You can't withhold information like that!"

"What… who?"

"I spoke to your DCI and he tells me you're responsible for the evidence file. I'm talking about the contradictions in the evidence against Jon Thorne; how did you think it would stay hidden? Why would you do such a thing? You know it's your responsibility to disclose *all* relevant documents, particularly those which undermine the prosecution or assist the defence."

Dumbstruck, Sue managed to say, "I've no idea what you're talking about, everything was disclosed."

He mutely waved a document at her. “The defence team have sent us a copy of this.”

“What is it?”

“A copy of an authority for Jon Thorne to go undercover to expose the Zodiac Club.”

“But that’s impossible… I didn’t know… I’ve never seen it.”

He handed the document to Sue and she scanned it. It was dated three weeks before the raid and signed by Chief Superintendent Irvine.

“But he was literally caught in the act with the others.”

“According to the statements of two of your officers there, he was fully dressed when they saw him and was in the bathroom as they came in. The two officers put him in a white suit, then sat him down with the others. Apparently, he was not involved at all. You must have known about it and tried to conceal this.”

Sue realised she had only seen Thorne after he had been put in a white forensic suit so was unable to refute that. She thought frantically, “The body worn video will show differently.”

“Several of the videos were corrupted, so are no good and none of the remaining show him.”

“There’s the forensic evidence, though.”

Damian lost his temper, “No there isn’t, he was the only one that was clean, another inconvenient fact you’ve overlooked.”

Sue now sounded desperate, her world was folding around her, “It’s all a cover-up. The evidence has obviously been tampered with. It's because Thorne is a Freemason, I'm sure of it."

"That's pathetic, don't blame your inadequacies on fantasy! I want you to know I've written to your chief constable complaining about your actions."

Sue tried to sound reasonable, "But that's not fair; Thorne is as guilty as hell."

"You may think that, but you still can't fabricate evidence and you can't hide inconvenient truths. You have no real evidence against him and your head of CID has said that he was there working undercover. Inspector Jon Thorne will be released as soon as possible."

With that he looked down and started to read. Sue had been dismissed from his office. She felt angry but impotent; what could she do now?

On the way back to the station, she phoned Steve to ask him to meet her in the coffee shop. As she drove through Leeston, Sue looked at all the people coming and going through the delightful town centre. How simple their lives must be, how uncomplicated with self-doubt. Could she be so wrong? Surely if Thorne were innocent, he would have said something? It's true, she came in on the raid afterwards and didn't know whether he was dressed or not, or whether he came from the bathroom. If two officers say he did, were they telling the truth, why would they lie?

What happened to the forensic evidence? Nobody had said anything to her before about there being no forensic evidence, was it an oversight or has there been more cover-up? Now she was feeling paranoid, was she turning into one of those crazy conspiracy theorists or had she been mistaken?

Sitting down with Steve in the Busy Bean coffee shop in the High Street, she posed her dilemma to him.

"Honestly, I think you're being a bit paranoid. Look Sue, I sat with you as you said that Irvine was a paedophile and you were wrong, now it's got to stop, enough is enough."

Sue was surprised at the vehemence of Steve's response.

He continued. "Look Sue, I get that you don't like Irvine, but this is an obsession, you can't blame him for all your problems."

"I'm not—" she started.

"Be happy with your success, you took down a major paedophile ring. You didn't know about Jon Thorne being undercover but that's because you kept Scotty Irvine out of the loop. You should have talked and worked together."

"Surely you're not falling for that bullshit, are you?" Sue was incredulous.

"Seriously Sue, drop it, it's not healthy."

Angry, Sue retorted, "I'll tell you what I'm dropping… you!" Before he could say anything else, she stormed out.

As Sue marched back to the station she thought about the situation. She knew that both Irvine and Thorne were Freemasons. She'd asked Sally, the intelligence analyst, to find out about the police officers who said they'd seen Thorne coming from the bathroom fully dressed. She would also look at the forensic evidence again.

Sue walked into the rear yard of the station where a number of police officers were busily coming and going. She was feeling good now, she knew she was right and had to find a way to expose the hypocrisy. She was disappointed in Steve but at last she knew where he stood.

Seeing Sally in her office, she smiled warmly, "News Sally?"

"Not good I'm afraid."

"Go on."

Sally collected her thoughts then started, "The two witnesses who allegedly saw Inspector Thorne leave the bathroom have altered their statements. Their originals have gone missing, but their statements are dated a day later and none of the other officers saw this. Oh, and as you guessed they're both known to be Freemasons. A couple of the body-worn videos are missing, unsurprisingly, they are the ones featuring Thorne. I don't know if the undercover surveillance authority is faked but there is no intelligence recorded and linked to it which I would normally expect. The forensic evidence was altered, I'm sure, but I can't prove it." Sally stopped as she realised that Sue had stopped listening and was staring intently past her with a frozen look on her face.

"What's that fucking bastard doing here?" Sue shouted, standing up quickly. Sally looked around and saw Inspector Jon Thorne walking along the corridor across the quadrangle on the other side of the building, going into the superintendent's office.

Sue jumped up and stormed around to the far side of the building. She barged straight into Superintendent Parfitt's office, "What's that paedophile bastard doing here?" she demanded.

"Now look here…" started the superintendent.

"Hello Sue." Thorne was smiling at her. "Haven't you heard, I'm innocent?"

Sue was furious, "That's just bullshit, like hell you're innocent. It's not finished!"

Superintendent Parfitt tried to exert some authority, "Detective Inspector Taylor, you can't come in here saying these things; Inspector Thorne is back at work because his name has been cleared by no less than Chief Superintendent Irvine. I hope that satisfies you?"

"Bollocks, he's the one behind this evil cover-up. He's a Freemason, they go to the same lodge. Irvine's covering up for his brother Mason and may well be a paedophile as well."

The superintendent was apoplectic; his whole world order was being challenged. "That's enough, get out of my office, take a break and come back when you can be reasonable!"

Sue stormed out again muttering to herself. She went to her office, grabbed her handbag, "Sorry Sally I've got to get away from here, I feel sick."

She strode out of the station, got into her car in the rear yard, lowered the roof, gunned the engine and then roared out onto the road.

After miles of driving through Leeston forest she had calmed down enough to think. She pulled into one of the many beauty spot car parks, where she could think things through. After a while she was resolved.

They will not get away with this. This is not over, she vowed.

The END